**The sexiest smile slid across Lyfe's lips
a fraction before his head descended.**

The two seconds it took for their mouths to connect
felt more like a lifetime, however, the reward was
well worth the wait. That underlining sweetness she
remembered was still there, but there was also so
much more.

More power.

More richness

This was not t⋯⋯⋯⋯⋯⋯⋯⋯⋯ a kiss of
a confident m⋯⋯⋯⋯⋯⋯⋯⋯⋯ things.

Weightless and suspended in what felt like an
alternative time and place. In his arms, she was grace
and beauty…and love. Just like that. As if there hadn't
been more than a dozen years since they'd been in
each other's arms melting from each other's kisses. At
the heart…there was still a strong foundation of love.

There was no room for reason and reality at this
moment. The past didn't matter and tomorrow was
just too far away for her to be concerned about. All
that mattered was right here and right now.

In no time at all, she was returning his kiss with the
same fierce hunger that he was trying to devour her
with. When she heard a deep growl rumble from his
chest, a surge of power surged through Corona. Her
ego couldn't help but inflate at the realization that she
still had power over him. She could do whatever she
wanted with him, right here and right now.

Books by Adrianne Byrd

Kimani Romance

She's My Baby
When Valentines Collide
To Love a Stranger
Two Grooms and a Wedding
Her Lover's Legacy
Sinful Chocolate
Tender to His Touch
Body Heat
Lovers Premiere
My Only Desire
A Christmas Affair

ADRIANNE BYRD

is a national bestselling author who has always preferred to live within the realms of her imagination, where all the men are gorgeous and the women are worth whatever trouble they manage to get into. As an army brat, she traveled throughout Europe and learned to appreciate and value different cultures. Now she calls Georgia home.

Ms. Byrd has been featured in many national publications, including *Today's Black Woman*, *Upscale* and *Heart and Soul*. She has also won local awards for screenwriting.

In 2006 Adrianne Byrd forged into the world of Street Lit as De'nesha Diamond. In 2008 she jumped into the young-adult arena writing as A.J. Byrd, and she is just hitting the women's fiction scene as Layla Jordan. She plans to continue creating characters that make people smile, laugh and fall in love.

A Christmas Affair

ESSENCE BESTSELLING AUTHOR

ADRIANNE BYRD

KIMANI
ROMANCE

KIMANI PRESS™

ISBN-13: 978-0-373-86234-4

A CHRISTMAS AFFAIR

Recycling programs
for this product may
not exist in your area.

Chapter 1

December 16, 1998
Dear Diary,
Tonight I, Corona Mae Banks, became a woman.
* We did it. I can't believe it, but we finally did it. After dating since the seventh grade, Lyfe Alton and I have finally done it. I'm no longer a girl but a woman. I wonder if everyone is going to notice a difference in me tomorrow. You know that they say that women walk differently after they...well, you know. (LOL) Anyway, I know that you want all the details—and it's not like I'd ever hide anything from you. So let me set the scene. As you know, Mom and Daddy headed out to Lagrange for Uncle Gary's hoedown Christmas party. They've been planning on it for weeks. Well, that left me to babysit Tess (like always). Once I got her to stop bumping her gums, and to actually go to sleep,*

I called Lyfe over. Let me tell you, he must have been circling the place because he was here in like three minutes flat.

It was still enough time for me to get a fire going in the fireplace, put the radio on the Quiet Storm—that's the program where they play nothing but slow jams—and sneak out one of Daddy's beers for him and one of Momma's wine coolers for me. When Lyfe tapped on the back sliding-glass door, I almost didn't hear him. But when I turned to see his tall frame (he's now six-four, can you believe it?) standing back there with snow flurries in his head, my heart melted. His shoulders looked like they were expanding a half an inch every day and there's just something about his milk-chocolate skin that makes me want to lick him every time I see him.

He's soooo fine—I swear that he could be a model or actor instead of a farmer. Heck. He could even be an architect. I've seen a lot of his drawings. He's really talented. He could really get out and see the world. I know that's what I want to do.

But a farmer? I still can't believe that's what he wants, but it's what his father does and he loves and admires his father. That breaks my heart just a little bit because that means he'll never leave Thomason, Georgia.

What's worse is that he'd want me to stay here with him. Don't get me wrong, I love Lyfe—always have and always will—but I can't wait for the day I leave this Mayberry-wannabe town. All I'd have to look forward to would be jarring peach pre-

serves, milking cows and birthing a whole village of babies. I mean, c'mon, Lyfe is the youngest of six. SIX!

Don't get me wrong. I now know that making seven babies with Lyfe will be rather...wonderful. *Sigh*

Okay. I'm getting ahead of myself. I was telling you about how our whole evening went down. First, I let my Boo into the house and then immediately took him over to the nice spot I had arranged in front of the fireplace. There, he asked a few questions about how it was putting up with my Energizer Bunny sister and when I started answering him, he started nibbling on my ear.

"Ooh, honey. That tickles." I giggled, but snuggled closer.

Lyfe responded by gathering me closer. Soon after, his lips stopped tickling and started feeling more like paradise. There's this spot just at the juncture of my neck and collarbone that is... giiiiiirrrrl. My toes are curling just thinking about it.

Before I know it, we're butt-naked and lying down on my father's God-awful bearskin rug. Well, at least it was soft. I can't say the same thing for Lyfe. (LOL)

My Boo was hard all over. And at his height, that's a lot of hard chocolate.

But Diary, he is soooo beautiful. His body deserves to be sculpted in granite and shown at all the major art museums for the world to just marvel at. Meanwhile, I'm the only woman who gets to feel the real deal. And let me tell you. It's something to *behold. And he smells so damn good—and clean. He's not loaded down with cologne or aftershave. He just smells like Ivory soap. Who knew that that could be a turn on?*

"Are you sure that you want to do this?" Lyfe asked. It was an awkward question to ask now that he had made it all the way to third base. Any other guy, particularly his older brothers, would "act" first and "talk" second—or just skip the talking all together.

This was it.

The big moment.

He was naked.

I was naked. But suddenly there was this massive lump in the center of my throat and I couldn't get any words out. To say, "yes," meant that I couldn't turn back.

At my silence, he quickly added, "I mean...I completely understand if you've changed your mind."

I heard what he was saying but his eyes and body were practically begging for me not to change my mind. I smiled up at him. "Are you nervous?"

"What? Who? Me?" he squeaked.

My lips stretched wider as I grew more relaxed. "Yeah—you."

"No. Of course not. Don't be silly," his voice squeaked so high this time that it cracked. He quickly coughed to cover it up, but the damage had already been done.

I struggled but I didn't laugh. "Actually, I kind of like it that you're a little nervous."

"You do?" he asked, astonished.

I nodded. "I'm nervous, too—and since this is our first time, why not be nervous together?"

A corner of Lyfe's lips hitched up and a good number of my butterflies settled down.

"Why not?" He turned his head and pressed a kiss against the palm of my hand before meeting my gaze with the same intensity I leveled on him.

My thick, wavy long hair was spread about my head like a black halo. "Do you know that your skin has a natural starburst of mahogany in your cheeks?"

"It does?"

He nodded, staring at me like I was the most beautiful thing he had ever seen.

"And I love your eyes," he said.

"You do?"

"Yeah. They get me every time. They're a beautiful mosaic of colors that could easily seduce any man."

"Stop it."

"No. I'm being serious," he insisted. "They're a burnt brown when you're angry, light sienna when you're happy and simmering amber when you're excited or turned on—just like they are right now."

I blushed so hard it felt like a Nevada heat wave.

The three previous times that we had gotten that far or close to "doing it," Lyfe claimed that he had already familiarized himself with every curve and dip on my luscious body. (That's what he called it—LUSCIOUS!)

He said that he liked my little black beauty mark beneath my right cheek and even the small scar above my right knee that I'd gotten on a bad slide into home base when I was nine years old. (Of course he was the one that was blocking the plate!) Anyway, he said that it was the small things that make me perfect. ME—PERFECT. I could just die.

Lyfe Alton is the most romantic man in all of Georgia.

"I'm sure," I said, panting and fluttering my lashes up at him. "I want to do this." There are just no words to describe how his strong chest felt against my breasts—other than paradise, but I've used that word already.

As much as he wanted to play it cool and act like he knew what he was doing, I knew that he was just as scared as I was. After all, this was his first time, too. Last year, he kept saying that he wanted to wait until he was married to have sex. It is, after all, what my father always preaches. But this year, the last thing we've been thinking about is what was being said on Sunday mornings.

He told me that he'd been dreaming of this moment for a long time. He'd practiced poetic words in front of the mirror like a love-sick puppy. He'd endured endless teasing from his five older brothers, usually after being caught talking—or doing other things—while imagining a night just like this one.

I cupped the other side of Lyfe's face with my hands. "Did you hear me? I'm really ready this time. I'm not going to change my mind."

Lyfe blinked and then struggled to swallow the boulder in his throat. This was really about to happen. I could feel his heart galloping inside his chest. How long had he dreamed of this moment? Since sixth, seventh grade? He said he couldn't remember anymore—just like he was struggling to remember all the pointers his older brothers had given him for when such a moment arrived.

"Condoms," he blurted. "We're supposed to use condoms." Panicked, he glanced around to where he'd kicked off his jeans. After scrambling to retrieve them, he pulled out a sleeve of four condoms—but they sort of looked...old.

"How long have those been in there?" I asked, frowning.

"Not long," he said, shrugging. "About a year... or so."

I don't know. I had a feeling that when we opened one that a dust cloud was going to float out.

A single worry line creased my forehead. Maybe it wasn't too late to back out—again. But I couldn't do that to him this time. After all, it wasn't the first time that we had gotten this far—not the first time that I'd told him that I was ready only to then stop him at the last possible second and announce that I'd changed my mind. Each time, I'd apologized profusely while he struggled to get his dick back into his pants so that he could limp home and take another cold shower. "You haven't changed your mind, have you?" I asked. He was taking a long time about opening the condom.

"Of course I haven't changed my mind," he

said. *"I just want to make sure that you're really, really sure this time."* He kept my gaze trapped as he vainly tried to swallow his own Adam's apple. *"Are you sure?"*

My lips spread into another smile while my hands reached for the condom. I boldly ripped the sucker open and then reached over and rolled it over his erection. My hands were trembling so bad. But as hard as he was, his dick still felt like smooth silk. (And it kept growing against my hand.) After fumbling around with it for about a minute, Lyfe finally reached down and helped roll the rest of it on. By that time, I'm wondering if I'm going to be able to fit all of him in. Surely something that big is going to hurt.

He must've heard my thoughts because the next thing Lyfe was saying was, *"I heard that it should only hurt for like a few seconds and then it goes away."*

A few seconds? Please. He was talking to a girl who's still afraid of needles. Again, I'm thinking about backing out, but a little voice inside of me keeps saying, *"You can do this."*

"You're still okay with this?"

"Has anyone ever told you that you ask too many questions?" I lean up and brush a kiss against his lips and then I'm just lost. (I've told you countless times before about how good Lyfe tastes, and tonight was no different.) At some point, I reach out and boldly wrap my hand around his throbbing dick, and I swear nearly every ounce of air fled that boy's lungs.

Suddenly I was filled with this amazing power.

It was like I could do anything and everything I wanted with him and he was going to let me do it. I can't even tell you all the things that raced through my mind, things that shocked and excited me at the same time.

While my sanity slipped a few notches, a sly smile hitched the corners of my lips. "Does that feel good?" I asked.

"I...I...Yes," he blurted. He closed his eyes and I could tell he was trying to will himself not to come before we even got started. We both had heard about that happening to a few of our friends on their first time. That's one humiliation that I think he could live without. But he continued to struggle with it while I slid my hands over his erection with long, fluid strokes.

To make matters worse, tears started glossing his eyes. Truly. I think it was feeling so good to him that he nearly started crying. Sure, it wouldn't have been the manly thing to do, but I can't help but think that it would've been sweet.
Sigh

Anyway. He didn't cry. But he definitely leveled the playing field when he reached down in between our bodies and slid one of his fingers through the soft hairs between my legs. Talk about being shocked. The air hissed out of my body like a flat tire. And when he started rubbing the pad of his finger against my pulsing clit, OH. MY. GOD!

I sucked in a quick breath and thrust my tits higher into the air. My reaction was clearly a pleasant surprise to him because he got this big ole smile on his face. So he stuck in another finger and started twirling them around even faster.

Each time his finger went from the tip of my clit to the base, my sighs heightened, my head tossed faster, and my thighs quivered like a 9.0 earthquake. Focusing on my pleasure allowed him to gain control over his own body—but not for long.

My hands stopped gliding and started pumping. In no time, his toes were curling. "How about this?" I asked. My competitive side had finally come out to play.

I never thought that sex could turn into a competition, but I'm here to testify that it definitely can. At first, I was compelled to win, but then Lyfe's fingers hit a certain spot and I was ready to wave a white flag of surrender and let him do whatever the hell he wanted to do with my body. I just didn't care.

Is that bad for me to say? Does that make me some kind of ho?

Then, within a snap of a finger, Lyfe started crying out, "Oh, God!"

I peeked out through my lashes to see that his eyes looked like they were ready to roll out the back of his head. Hell, I'm not even too sure that he was even breathing.

I know that Lyfe is no stranger to the art of masturbation (he's told me plenty of times about how his mother has nearly walked in on him). But I have a feeling that his large, heavy hands are a poor substitute for my soft, delicate ones, which were currently driving him wild.

"You like this, don't you, baby?" I asked, lean-

ing up and brushing a kiss against his neck. "*Tell me how it feels.*"

"*It...feels...wonderful,*" *he panted.* "*Just don't... stop.*" *He planted his hands on both sides of my head and started to rock his hips, as his cock slid in and out of my hand.*

"*I'm not going to stop this time,*" *I whispered against his ear.* "*I promise.*" *With that, I rained more kisses down the column of his neck and then blew a long steady stream of air against his ear.*

"*Oh, God, yes.*" *Lyfe quickly sucked in a deep breath and reminded himself aloud not to come too soon again.*

I pulled back, allowing Lyfe to unglue his eyes from the back of his head.

"*I'm ready,*" *I said.* "*I want my first time to be with you.*" *I leaned up again, keeping my eyes open as I brushed my lips against his.* "*Tonight.*"

While still holding his gaze, I glided his erection closer to the center of my body.

"*Is this it?*" *he asked, jamming his cock dead into my thigh.*

"*Ow. No.*" *I shook my head and then tried not to laugh out loud.* "*That is definitely not it.*"

He struggled to reposition himself while I take hold of his cock again and tried to get him a little closer. But before I could get him to the right spot, he surged his hips forward again and jammed up against the wrong hole.

"*OWWW.*" *I nearly jumped up off the floor.*

"*Sorry. Sorry.*"

The worried look on his face was just priceless.

We tried it again, but I warned him, "Don't do anything until I get you at the right spot."

Sheepishly, he nodded and waited like a good boy until I eased the head of his cock between my lower lips. Then...this was it. The big moment. I drew in a deep breath, wanting to savor the last few seconds of my virginity. I wanted to be cognizant of the fact that I was going from being a girl to a woman.

"Now?" Lyfe asked, jittery with anticipation. Even his eyes looked fever pitched.

"Now," I told him and then planted a big wet kiss on him.

He surged forward.

"Ahh." I tore my lips away just as quickly and sank my nails deep into his shoulder blades.

Lyfe hissed in his own shock and froze. "Did I do something wrong?" For a few seconds, he remained completely and utterly still, except for his throbbing cock pulsing inside of me.

I wasn't sure if I was okay or not. I was halfway embarrassed and halfway scared that I needed a doctor. I thought he might've broken something.

At long last, he pulled his head up to search my face. "Are you all right? Do you want to stop?"

If I said yes, I knew that he would be in an iced shower for at least a week. He continued to hold his breath until I mustered up my courage. "N-no. I'm okay," I panted.

"Are you sure?" The minute the question was out, I could tell that he wanted to smack himself over the head. Why keep looking a gift horse in the mouth?

I eased on a soft smile and then slid my hands down to his strong, muscled ass. "I'm absolutely positive," I whispered. Clearly, it was my turn to take charge. I dipped and rolled my hips, easing him in deeper.

Lyfe struggled to keep his eyes from rolling to the back of his head again. Instead, he kept his gaze locked on mine as he started to move inside of me again. Somehow, in some unexplainable way, my body heat penetrated his soul. At least it felt that way as wave after wave of pleasure washed over us. Our hips moved in sync and, within a few glorious strokes, we were filling the living room with soft sighs and moans. We'd done it. We'd officially made the leap from mere high school boyfriend and girlfriend to full-fledged lovers, and it was clear that neither one of us was sorry.

While we rode high, I knew that this was a moment to be savored and forever etched into our memories. I watched as the flittering light from the fireplace danced across his dewy skin, and gloated while his lower lip quivered between strokes and low baritone moans.

"Ohh, Lyfe," I panted. I was more in love with him at that moment than I've ever been. Our pants and moans blended together like a beautiful duet.

Soon after, he swept more kisses down the column of my neck while whispering, "I love you so much, Corona Mae. I'm yours forever. I'm here, baby. Tell me what you want—what you need."

Hell, all I needed was for him to keep doing what he was doing.

I rolled my hips a third and then a fourth time. I was getting warmer and wetter with each stroke. It seemed like a whole new world was opening up to me and I was greedy to see and feel more. Is this how it always is with sex? Or am I feeling these things because I'm in love with Lyfe?

"Whoa...whoa...wait...wait..." Lyfe gasped and then bit his lower lip. I could tell that it was just an attempt to regain control of his deteriorating willpower. Mercifully, I eased up and gave him all of fifteen seconds to try to regroup. As he opened his eyes, I was once again overwhelmed not only by the passion flickering in them but by the intensity of love that danced there as well.

With renewed confidence, Lyfe surged his hips forward and watched my expressions with fascination. His strokes were gentle, but he made sure that they grew longer and deeper.

"How does it feel, baby?" Lyfe asked. His lips stretched wide as he watched me struggle to answer. After a few more strokes, his cockiness evaporated and his toes curled tight. "Oh, God," he groaned and then dropped his head against the crook of my neck where he breathed in my scent and lazily dusted more kisses across my collar bone and then down the valley between my breasts.

"Mmm. You smell and taste like honey and cinnamon."

"Oh, Lyfe," I moaned, digging my nails into the tender flesh of his muscled shoulders. "Please, don't stop."

"I have no intentions of ever stopping. You're mine now."

Diary, I felt like I was really losing my mind. But through the fuzzy mesh of my eyelashes I could see that in his quest to give me pleasure, he was steadily marching himself right over a cliff. Things started tingling in places that I can't even risk writing to you. But just know that it was all so wonderful.

Lyfe's breath came in short, choppy puffs. Before long, he was completely and utterly lost.

I started slipping into a vortex of pleasure. It became increasingly hard to keep air in my lungs while my body was being assaulted with all these wonderful sensations. Our moans grew into a crescendo that drowned out Mariah Carey's "All I Want for Christmas is You" playing on the radio.

I cried out and then started trembling violently. Above me, Lyfe unleashed a growl that sounded like something out of the jungles of Africa. A half a second later there was a bright light and then we were floating in a galaxy of stars. It was the most beautiful thing ever.

Collapsing in a heap, he locked his arms around me while I rolled over and peppered kisses across his sweat-slicked forehead. "Thank you," I whispered.

He fluttered his eyes open. "That's kind of an odd thing to thank me for, don't you think?"

I blushed and then was rewarded with more kisses. "Thank you," I repeated.

He just stamped on a silly smile and said, "You're welcome. Feel free to ask me to do this with you again any time. Your wishes are my command."

I giggled. "How about now?"

He blinked. "Now, now?"

"Yeah." I smirked. "That is...if you're UP for it."

We both looked down at his growing cock.

"I don't think that is going to be a problem," he said. The front door banged open.

From the corner of my eye, I saw a pair of skinny legs racing up the stairs. (Tess! She probably saw the whole thing!) But that wasn't our main problem. Mom and Dad came back home early.

"Damn it, Adele! It's colder than a witch's titties out here," my father declared, swiping off his hat.

"Just be glad that we were able to get back before they closed the roads, Rufus," Momma said. "Just get yourself on in by the fire and I'll fix you some..." They froze as their eyes finally landed on the scene before the fireplace.

Lyfe and I were equally frozen.

Then, finally, Daddy thundered, "WHAT IN THE HELL IS GOING ON IN HERE?"

"Uh...evening, Mr. and Mrs. Banks," Lyfe fumbled out. Hell. I don't think he could think of anything else to say.

But Daddy brought us back to reality real quick.

"Adele, where's my damn gun?"

That was cue enough for Lyfe to jump his butt up and make a grab for his clothes. The rest of the *sleeve of condoms sliding across the floor didn't make things any better. Momma looked faint.*

Daddy pulled out his shotgun from his gun cabinet next to the grandfather clock.

"Wait, Daddy no!" I yelled, jumping up—naked as the day I came into the world.

"Father in heaven," Daddy roared and then took aim.

"Rufus, baby, wait!"

Lyfe tried to cram one leg through his boxers but ended up tipping over too much and tripping over the head of the bearskin rug. It was a good thing too because Daddy got off his first shot.

POW!

The buckshot grazed Lyfe's ass cheeks. "Oww!"

"Rufus, honey, don't kill the boy!"

"Damn it, Adele. I told you those damn Alton boys were no damn good!"

POW!

Lyfe scrambled low on the floor, figuring it was best to try to dodge behind the coffee and end tables.

"Coming up in here and disrespecting my daughter!"

POW!

"My daughter!"

POW!

"My house!"

POW!

"Daddy, stop," I wailed.

"You hush up now, child," Daddy barked. "I'll deal with you later."

*Lyfe made a dash toward the back glass door.
Unfortunately, the next buckshot shattered the
damn thing before he could reach it, but that didn't
stop him from diving straight through it and out
into the Georgia snowstorm—in his birthday suit
with Daddy still hollering and chasing after him...*

Buuuuuzzzzzzz!

Corona Banks jumped a foot out of her chair and then
slammed her diary that she'd been reading shut. It took
another half a second for her to realize that the buzzing
was coming from her desk phone. Not wanting the call
to go to voicemail, she quickly snatched up the receiver.
"Banks Artists Agency, this is Chloe."

"There you are! What on earth are you still doing at
the office?" Margo, her assistant, hissed into the line.
"You're supposed to be here at Rowan's place for the *E!*
interview. We're all waiting."

Corona sprung up out of her chair. How on earth had
she forgotten about that? She glanced over at the calen-
dar and there in bold black lettering was indeed this afternoon's interview. "I'm on my way. Stall them." She
slammed the phone and then glanced back down at the
stack of diaries on her desk. She needed to find a new
hiding space. The floorboard that she had concealing
her stash had been suspiciously moved, and she had a
growing fear that someone had found her treasure trove.

With no more time to think about the possible spy,
she jammed the books back into her briefcase and
rushed out of her New York office. She had more important things to deal with right now than daydreaming
about a decade-old love that had never had a chance.

Chapter 2

Corona rushed up the stairs to the SoHo apartment in a pair of fresh-out-of-the-box Louboutins. While she went through the fruitless exercise of berating herself for running late, she had long ago accepted the fact that in all likelihood she would be late for her own funeral. It wasn't that she was lazy or didn't plan ahead of time—she just had a tardiness gene somewhere in her DNA. At least that was her excuse and she was sticking to it.

"Is everyone still here?" she asked Margo the moment she bolted through the front door.

Relief washed over Margo's face at the sight of her boss. "Oh, thank God. The film crew has been here for over an hour. They were just talking about doing the interview without you." She rushed over to help Corona out of her A-line Mischka coat to reveal her snow-white Gucci pantsuit. "Nice," Margo said, her eyes widening appreciatively at Corona's immaculate fashion sense.

"Thanks. I can't have my fiancé show me up. Call me vain."

"All right, Vain," Margo said, shooing her toward the living room. "You just get in there before Rowan starts reenacting his Hamlet soliloquies from his Shakespeare in the park days."

Corona smiled. No one loved a camera more than Rowan James. Heralded as this generation's most bankable movie star, Rowan lived to be in the public eye. He instinctively knew his best angle and lighting at any given moment. While Corona thought of herself as attractive, she couldn't say that she and cameras had the same love affair.

Inevitably, her plump apple cheeks would look too big or her doe-shaped eyes would make her look like a deer caught in the headlights. It was the oddest thing. When people met her, they would always toss out the backhanded compliment that she was more beautiful in person.

"Hurry," Margo kept shooing her. "He's getting ready to thank God and the Academy."

Corona laughed, brushed her thick hair behind her ears, and marched into the apartment's large, open living room with a ready-made smile. "Hello, everyone. I'm so sorry to have kept you all waiting," she announced, with her voice all syrupy sweet. "Things were crazy at the office."

Rowan James turned his dark head, and his glowing blue eyes lit up at the sight of her. "There's my baby now." He stood up and drew Corona into his arms before brushing a sweetheart kiss against her upturned face. "Glad you could make it. I hope this isn't a dry run of what you're planning to do to me at the altar," he joked with just a tinge of seriousness.

"We'll just have to wait and see," Corona joked back with a playful wink.

K. D. Hardaway, a trailblazing celebrity reporter with womanly curves and high volume, corkscrew curls, popped up out of her seat and thrust out her hand. "The lady of the hour. We're so happy that you could finally join us. I personally have been dying to meet you."

Corona went to accept the woman's handshake, but at the last minute, the exuberant woman abandoned the idea and instead threw her arms around her like they were long lost friends.

"You know the whole world is hating on you now, right?" the woman informed her.

Corona didn't but she supposed that she should be grateful for the update. When she pulled back, K.D. kept a tight hold of her right hand. "Let's see the rock, honey. *Bam!*" The reporter dipped her knees and dramatically flung her head back. "Well, all right now! Ha!" She turned toward her lone cameraman. "Ed, we don't need a close-up on this one. I think the folks down in Texas are busy trying to get the glare of this diamond out of their eyes right now."

Corona smiled sheepishly while Rowan swung his arm around her shoulders and thrust out his chest. "Nothing but the best for my Chloe." He pried her hand from the reporter and then pressed a kiss just above her ring. "Honest to God, she's the best thing that has ever happened to me," he boasted.

K.D.'s perfectly arched brows damn near stretched to the top of her hairline as she gave them snaps in a Z-formation. "Well, all right now!"

Rowan laughed and pulled Corona even closer.

"So the entertainment world has their new power couple," K.D. announced, winking into the camera. "It's all good with me. It's about time someone knocked Will and Jada off their throne."

"Oh, I don't know about that," Corona said, shaking her head. "My work is behind the cameras."

"Exactly! That's where all the power is, girlfriend. Don't play." She held up her hand, signaling for a high five.

Corona gave Rowan a look that asked whether this chick was for real or a caricature of every sister-girl role that she had ever seen in rom-com movies rolled into one.

He responded with a quick shrug.

"Don't leave me hanging, girlfriend."

Corona finally threw her hand up against K.D.'s which caused her entire arm of silver bracelets to start jiggling like crazy while she cheesed with a smile that could rival The Joker's.

"So while we still have a few minutes, why don't you tell our audience how you two met? Was it love or lust at first sight? Give us the dirt."

Corona opened her mouth to answer, but Rowan quickly cut her off.

"I'm not ashamed to say that I felt something the first time I laid eyes on her. Chloe was like a ray of sunshine, and that's saying a lot in this business."

K.D. shifted back to Corona. "Is that how you felt, too? Wait. What am I saying? Who wouldn't have fallen head over heels for this gorgeous hunk, huh?"

"Well…" Corona hesitated with a nervous look over at Rowan.

"You got to be kidding me." K.D.'s traveling brows had now blended into her curly hair.

Corona opened her mouth, only to be cut off once again by her overeager fiancé, who undoubtedly wanted to put a nicer spin on the story.

"Actually, it was probably *not* one of my best nights when we met," Rowan laughed and then tossed a wink toward the camera.

"Oh?" The reporter edged closer, sensing a juicy story was coming her way.

"Yeah, I guess you can say that I was being a bit of a bad boy at a bar," Rowan answered sheepishly. "As everyone out there in TV land knows, I went through quite an ugly breakup last year."

K.D. nodded her head sympathetically, just like Corona imagined everyone else at home was doing right now. The entertainment world had been riveted for the past two years over Rowan's love affair with Hollywood's hottest sex kitten, Danica Foxx. Glossy tabloid magazines had made a fortune planting their faces on every cover in the western hemisphere. But, predictably, with all the media scrutiny, a couple that hot was bound to implode.

And they did. Quite spectacularly. Danica cheated on him. All that was missing was a set of golf clubs and a small library of lurid text messages to complete Rowan's humiliation. But it was Danica's announcement two days later that she was engaged to the movie star whom she did the cheating with that crushed Rowan.

"Anyway, I was sort of drowning my sorrows at the bottom of a Jack Daniel's bottle, tossing back one shot after another when I looked up and there she was."

Rowan turned and smiled at Corona. "An angel. A vision in white."

Corona rolled her eyes at the way he was spinning their story.

"Sounds like you made quite an impression," K.D. said.

"Yea, me." Corona twirled her finger in the air with a breezy laugh before thinking better of it. Realizing that she needed to clean up her act a bit, she tried to explain. "You don't understand. By the time me and my assistant, Margo, had made our way to the bar, Rowan and his new buddy Jack Daniels weren't getting along so well."

Rowan tossed the camera another wink.

"Our first meeting happened because I felt sorry for him for not being able to sit on a barstool," Corona continued, finally starting to laugh at the memory. "Margo and I had a fun-filled evening lugging Mr. Blockbuster here back to his hotel. The whole time he kept telling me how perfect I was for a part in his next film. It was so cliché. Trust me."

"Cliché or not, clearly whatever you did worked," the reporter concluded.

"Not really," Rowan laughed. "They dumped me on my bed—"

"More like he passed out," Corona corrected.

"And when I woke the next morning, I was convinced I'd only dreamt her up." He laughed and leaned over to give her another kiss. "Imagine my surprise when I saw her on the movie set later that evening talking to another star on the film. I couldn't believe my eyes. I was convinced that it had to be fate."

"And I thought that I must have made someone mad in a past life," Corona joked.

K.D. continued to look astonished. "You're kidding me?"

"See why I'm marrying her? Anyone else in this town would've called the tabloids and made a quick buck."

Sharp as a tack, K.D. cut in, "But it still proved to be beneficial to her. After all, she did sign you to the Banks Artists Agency, did she not?"

"Only after I tracked her down and begged her to represent me," he said slyly.

"Really?"

"Well, what else could I do? She refused to go out with me."

The reporter turned her incredulous eyes back toward Corona. "You're kidding. You actually told the number one box office star in the world that you wouldn't go out with him?"

Corona's apple cheeks darkened with embarrassment. "No. I told the drunken guy that threw up in my shoes that I didn't want to go out with him. I can forgive a lot of things, but ruining a pair of my favorite Jimmy Choos took divine intervention to forgive."

Rowan smiled. "But the more she resisted, the more I just had to have her."

"Ahh. So you're a man who loves a challenge," K.D. said.

"You can definitely say that," he said, pressing another kiss to the back of Corona's hand and then leaning over and stealing a slow kiss for all of America to see. When he finally pulled back, he declared, "I'm the happiest man in the world right now."

Chapter 3

Over eight hundred miles south, in Thomason, Georgia, Lyfe Alton cocked his head up at the thirteen-inch television in Parker's Service Station and tried to keep his drive-thru dinner down while he watched Corona Mae and superstar Rowan James smile and laugh in front of the cameras. Behind him, the small gas station's door opened and jingled its bell.

"What in the hell is taking you so long in here?" Hennessey thundered, strutting up behind his younger brother and then smacking his heavy hand against his back. When Lyfe didn't respond, he turned his head up at the television set to see what had caught his brother's attention. "Hey! Ain't that—"

"Yes," Lyfe droned and then folded his arms.

Hennessey twisted up his face. "And ain't that—"

"Yes," Lyfe clipped out again, hoping his brother

would catch a hint and shut the hell up. Of course he didn't.

"Well, what in the hell are they talking about?" Hennessey asked and then glanced around until he saw the station's owner behind the counter. "Yo, Parker. Can you turn this up?"

Lyfe closed his eyes and then drew in a long, steady breath. "C'mon. Let's just go ahead and go." He turned, but Hennessey's gigantic hand locked on his shoulder and held him in place.

"Wait. Wait. Hold up."

Behind the counter, old man Parker found his remote control and turned up the television set...

"Wow. I really am impressed," the reporter with the wild hair said. She paused for a beat to allow the cameraman to zoom in on the engaged couple glancing lovingly at each other. "So let's get to the nitty-gritty. When is the big day?"

"Christmas Day," Rowan said, beaming. "Believe it or not, I've always dreamed of getting married on that day."

"So did I," Lyfe argued back at the screen. When he realized what he'd said aloud, he turned to his older brother. "Are you about ready to go?"

"Shh," Hennessey said. "I'm trying to hear this."

"Well, ain't that about—"

"Parker, turn it up some more," his brother shouted. "Motor mouth here won't shut the hell up."

Lyfe snapped his jaw shut while his two brows crashed together. *Now if that doesn't beat all.* Grudgingly, he turned his head back toward the screen just as the station's doorbell jingled again.

"Afternoon, Parker," a familiar lyrical voice floated in.

Lyfe and Hennessey craned their necks around to watch willowy and leggy Tess stroll into the station.

Old man Parker lifted up the bill of his trucker's hat and tossed the woman that was young enough to be his great-granddaughter a wink. "How you doing today, Miss Tess?"

"Oh, I'm doing fine," she sighed, adding an extra *humph!* to her hips as she sashayed over to the counter. "I'm just looking for something to get into. You know how it is." She handed over a pile of lottery tickets. "Daddy wants you to check his numbers."

"Sure. No problem," Parker said, jumping right to work.

Lyfe snickered. He had a feeling that if Tess asked the man to jump off the roof of the building while singing *Old McDonald* he would do it. The man was that smitten—just like most men that had the fortune or misfortune to cross her path were.

Catching the sound of Lyfe's chuckle, Tess finally turned her bored gaze in his and his brother's direction. She immediately lit up.

"Well, well. If it ain't the Alton boys." Tess's beautiful smile grew bigger as she pushed away from the counter and strutted her way toward them. "Good Lord. All these chocolate muscles up in here. A sister might pass out."

Hennessey laughed, mainly because Tess was as big a flirt as he was. "Don't worry. If you faint, know that I got you."

Lyfe rolled his eyes. He was going to have to take another look at his brother's birth certificate and double-check that his middle name wasn't "Corny."

When she drew closer, her eyes widened. "Oh, my

God…is that…Lyfe Alton? What on earth are you doing back in town?"

"Hello, Tess," he said, tilting his head. "I'm on a little sabbatical from my architecture firm, so I came down to spend a couple of months with the folks."

"Sabbatical, huh? Tired of living in the big city and thinking about coming back home?"

He shrugged to avoid answering.

Tess's eyes roamed over him. He felt naked. He wondered if he should grab something to cover his private parts just in case she could see through his clothes.

"You know I never told you, but I used to have the biggest crush on you back in the day."

"Is that right?" he said, straight-faced. The fact that Tess looked so much like her sister was beginning to make his chest hurt.

"Uh, huh." Tess nodded. "But you were so stuck on Corona Mae that I don't think you ever noticed any other girl in town."

"He sure in the hell didn't," Hennessey said.

Lyfe gave his brother a hard glare that served as a final warning.

"What?" Hennessey asked, shrugging his shoulders. "It's the truth."

Only Tess picked up on his discomfort. "So where is the rest of the litter?" she asked. "Everybody knows that the Alton six-pack travels together."

Lyfe shook his head as he looked her over again. "Like everything else, times change."

Tess settled her hands on her hips as she tossed him a flirtatious wink. "Indeed." She started to say something more when her gaze suddenly cut toward the suspended television set. "Is that—"

"Yep," Hennessey said. "Looks like your older sister is still doing big things up in New York."

"Parker, can you turn this up?"

"You got it!" Parker said, hitting the volume on the remote until people outside were likely able to hear the television set.

Lyfe groaned. But instead of leaving, like he should've done, his attention returned to the screen. Why not? He was a glutton for punishment, wasn't he?

"Tess, honey. What the hell is taking you so long in here?" Rufus Banks thundered and then added to his old friend, "Yo, Parker, what's up?"

"Nothing much. Just running your tickets through the machine here."

Lyfe stiffened. He couldn't help it. Things between him and Mr. Banks had never healed since the night he'd walked in on him and his daughter naked in their living room. Bullets flying at you in the middle of a snowstorm generally tended to have a lasting negative effect on a person.

The men's gazes crashed.

"What the hell are you doing back here?" Rufus barked.

"You'll never believe who's on television, Daddy," Tess said, interrupting a potential war.

Rufus grudgingly shifted his attention away from Lyfe and followed her finger that was pointing to the television. A millisecond later, a genuine smile carved its way into the center of his gray beard while he, too, strolled over to stand beneath the screen. "Well, look at Corona Mae all gussied up. What's going on?"

Hennessey shrugged. "It appears you're finally about to get yourself a son-in-law."

"Say what?" Rufus squinted up at the screen.

"I'll give you a hint," Tess said, folding her arms beneath her small breasts. "Guess who's coming to dinner."

Rufus's eyes bugged out. "What? That white boy right there?"

Lyfe gave him a lopsided smile. "Well, look at it this way. It's not me."

The men's gazes locked again and another layer of tension was added between them. When Lyfe was younger, the look Rufus Banks was giving him would've been enough for him to trip over himself and scramble home. But fourteen years later, Lyfe was an intimidating man himself.

"Come on, Hennessey. Let's get out of here."

Chapter 4

The minute their wedding announcement segment ended on the entertainment channel, Corona powered off the television then jumped out of bed and raced toward the bathroom. "Oh, God. I think that I'm going to be sick."

"Hey!" Rowan said from his side of the bed, as he lowered the script that he was reading. "I thought it was a very nice interview."

Corona ignored him and dropped onto her knees next to the toilet bowl and waited for her dinner to make an encore appearance. But instead her stomach bent and turned like it was playing its own private game of Twister.

"Are you all right in there?"

She gagged and coughed but still nothing came up. "Yeah." She sniffed and hung her head low so that her voice echoed in the porcelain chamber. "I'm fine." In her mind, she replayed the syrupy sweet interview and felt another violent jerk in the center of her stomach.

What if my family saw it?

"You're worried about your family," Rowan said.

Corona jerked her head up to see her freshly minted fiancé leaning against the bathroom doorframe. He looked so studious in his wire-rimmed frames, and a hunk of his black hair flopped over his left eye. Then again, the man really didn't have a bad angle on him.

"And don't bother lying to me," Rowan warned before she could think of a good lie. "I can tell that you're worried about them learning about our engagement in the media before we get a chance to tell them in person."

"Well—"

"Then let's just fly down there and tell them. Get it out of the way. I don't understand what the big deal is," he said, shaking his head. "I'm starting to feel like the black sheep or something."

Corona stretched up a single brow.

Rowan coughed and cleared his throat. "Okay. Bad choice of words."

"You think?" Corona dragged herself off the floor and then quickly rummaged through her medicine cabinet for her beloved bottle of Excedrin.

"Okay. Then let's just call them."

"We will," she said.

"When?"

"Soon." It was all that she could offer.

Rowan's steady gaze trapped her. "Is it because I'm white?"

"What? Don't be ridiculous."

"Come on. You can tell me. I'm a big boy."

"No." She grabbed a Dixie cup and quickly filled it

with water so she could down her precious two pills. "It's not that."

"But it's something…right?"

Cornered, Corona prolonged swallowing her pills by holding them and the water in her cheeks longer than necessary.

When she didn't respond, Rowan tossed up his hands. "Fine. Fine. I can take a hint. Believe it or not, I don't need a brick building to fall on my head, you know. You don't want to tell your parents right now. I'll step back and respect that—but we're going to have to tell them sooner or later."

Corona sucked in a deep breath, but she didn't answer him.

"All right. You know what? I'm going to head back to my place to study this script," he said, turning around. "We begin shooting soon and I need to concentrate."

Finally swallowing her pills, Corona followed him. "Whoa. Wait, Rowan. You don't have to do that."

"Actually, I do." He completed his march over to the bed and started shoving his things into the leather duffle bag that he usually brought when there was a possibility of him being able to stay the night.

Corona sighed at having made a complete mess of this night. But, then again, didn't this just fit the MO of how she generally screwed things up when it came to relationships? "Rowan—"

"I'll call you tomorrow," he said, blazing toward her and stopping briefly to peck a light kiss against the top of her head. That was definitely a sign that she'd screwed this evening up.

"Row—" She reached to stop him, but he was already

halfway to the bedroom door and she was left grasping at air. "All right. Goodnight then."

"'Night." He slipped out of the door and left her to listen to his heavy footsteps as they rushed down the staircase.

In the back of Corona's mind, she had the fleeting desire to chase after him. But if she succeeded in doing that, what was she going to give as a better explanation as to why she wasn't ready to introduce him to her family?

No, she wasn't the only transplant from Georgia roaming the streets of Manhattan. But she was pretty sure that the other movers and shakers in the concrete jungle didn't have fathers that proudly proclaimed winning the top prize in the Southern Select Show Pig Championship or chased the boyfriends they didn't like with a shotgun and forced them to marry their daughters.

Call it a hunch.

Oh, she loved her parents. Really. She did.

She just loved them more when they remained in Thomason, Georgia. What was it they said? *Absence makes the heart grow fonder?* That was certainly the case with her and her family.

Hell, she'd forgotten to ask Rowan about her diaries—or accuse him of finding and reading them.

Riiiiiinnnng!

Corona jumped and then jerked her head toward the phone on the nightstand next to the bed. "Rowan." Maybe he wasn't so mad at her after all. A side of her lips quirked up. He might even be standing outside the building, wanting to say how much he hated how things had ended on a weird note between them tonight. After all, Rowan was a strong advocate of not going to bed angry.

The weight of the world lifted off her shoulders. She raced over to the phone and snatched it up with her apology cresting her lips before she even got the receiver to her ear. "Baby, I'm so sorry."

"Well, it's about time you admitted it!"

Her face twisted. "Who is this?"

"Damn. You don't even recognize the voice of your little sister anymore?"

Corona slammed her eyes closed and groaned. "Tess."

"Wow. What a way to make a girl feel special, *Chloe*," her sister sniped. "What a ridiculous name. I'm calling you Corona. You were named after our grandmother, and you should be proud of that."

"I am proud, it's just…"

"Country. And country doesn't work in the big city."

"Can we please not argue about this?"

"Fine. I called to ask why I had to find out about your getting married to Mr. Action-Pack on that little thingy we call down here 'the boob tube.'"

Corona's heart sank. "You saw that?"

"As a matter of fact, I did. I watched it standing in the middle of Parker's Gas Station with Daddy and… Lyfe Alton."

"What?" Corona blinked and felt like she was being swept back into a time machine. What were the chances of Lyfe popping up on the same day that she had just been reading in her diary about their first time together?"

"Shocking, isn't it?"

"To say the least," Corona agreed. Her brain started

churning out so many questions that she didn't know which one to ask first. "What...why...how?"

"Exactly what I asked," Tess said, picking up on her sister's shorthand.

"Well, what did he say?"

"Not much. Really. Only that he was in town on sabbatical."

Chloe nearly swallowed her tongue.

"Just imagine if you'd just come home for the holidays like I begged you. Who knows, maybe you two would've run into each other."

She swallowed. "Like that would have been a good thing." Still, she couldn't stop herself from imagining what such a chance encounter would've been like. *Awkward. Painful. Explosive.*

"How long is he in town for?" Chloe asked, trying to sound casual.

"Don't know. Didn't ask."

"*You* didn't ask?" she said, shocked.

"Why do you say it like that?"

"Because I've never known you to miss an opportunity to get all up in someone else's business," Chloe answered honestly. "Never."

"Well, we all were a little distracted with you and Rowan James trying to inhale each other's faces on national television. Really. Next time, try just getting a room."

"Ohmigod. Lyfe saw that?"

Tess clucked. "With you being in the industry, I figured that you knew how cameras worked. They broadcast to millions of people—even to ones who are just standing in a gas station."

Corona felt like she might need to make another run to the bathroom.

"When exactly were you planning to tell us that you're marrying a white boy?"

"Don't say it like that. What difference does it make what color he is?"

"I don't care what color he is, but people like a heads-up."

"I know. I know. I'll call them."

"Uh-huh. Right," Tess challenged. "Looks to me like you were planning to avoid the issue by doing what you always do, run away."

"Not funny."

"It wasn't meant to be."

"That's not fair," Chloe argued.

"But it is true."

Silence.

"See? You may be good at running your little business up there."

"Little?"

"But when it comes to family issues, you race out of the kitchen before the stove gets too hot. Talk to Daddy. It is waaaay past time for you two to settle y'all's issues."

"I know. I know." And she did know. Things had never been the same between them since she had left Georgia the way she did. "I'll talk to him. I promise."

"I've heard that before," Tess pressed.

"Okay. Is there another reason you called—other than to make me feel like crap?"

"Nope. I just wanted to check that off my to-do list."

"Great. Fine. Consider it done." She was tempted to slam the phone down, but she still had more questions about Lyfe that kept her from introducing Tess to Mr. Dial Tone.

"So. There's nothing else you want to ask me?" Tess said, sounding like she knew exactly why her sister hadn't slammed the phone down.

Silence.

"Say…anything about Lyfe Alton that you're curious to know?"

"How…did he look? I mean—"

"Honey, let me tell you—that brother is sooooo freaking fine that the sheriff needs to be handing out tickets." Tess roared to life. "I ain't even lying. Tall as a mountain, muscle like POW! and POW! I mean, arms and thighs—but not like those gym muscleheads. I would give my right arm to drip some strawberry sauce all over Mr. Man's body."

"Have you forgotten just who in the hell you're talking to?" Chloe snapped.

Tess cleared her throat. "Uhm…actually, yes." Cough. "Sorry about that. But, Corona, I'm telling you. Out of the Alton six-pack, baby boy ain't a baby no more."

"Thanks."

"I mean it. He's—"

"I said thanks. I get it. He's good looking. I kind of figured that much."

"Can I have him?" Tess asked meekly.

"What?"

"Look, I know that there's some unwritten rule about dating your sister's exes. But hell. You don't come around here no more anyway."

"I'm about to hang up on you."

"Is that a 'no'?"

"Hell yes, it's a 'no,'" Corona thundered. If her sister was standing in front of her right now, she was certain that she would have wrapped her hands around the child's neck and squeezed until she was the same color as a Smurf.

"Well, I don't see what the big damn deal is. You're about to get married and expand the family. Don't you want to see me happy?"

"You so much as bat an eyelash at Lyfe, I'll see you six feet under."

"Ooh. Testy. Could it be that you're not quite over your first love?"

"I'm hanging up now."

"That's all right. I know how to call back."

"You'll get the answering machine," she warned. *When in the hell is that Excedrin going to kick in?*

"I'd imagine that if you really cared about Lyfe's feelings that you probably wouldn't have left him standing at the altar."

"There was no altar," she grudgingly pointed out.

"Fine. You wouldn't have left him standing in our backyard in a suit that barely fit and with Daddy pointing a shotgun at his back."

"Oh, God, are you ever going to let me live that down?"

"Uhm, no. Can't say that I will," Tess said. "What you did was foul."

"Well, excuse me. Shotgun weddings went out about a hundred years ago. My ditching Thomason to come live in New York was the right thing to do and you know it."

"Humph!"

"Fine. I'm the bad guy. I get it. Foolish me. I thought

that you only called to remind me of that on Christmas and my birthday."

"Consider today a special occasion."

"Your snarky sarcasm is getting old."

"And believe it or not, our worlds don't revolve around you. Other people have feelings, you know?"

"Yes. I do know that!"

"Do you? Is that why you were all up on the television telling the world that you're getting married but you didn't even find time to call your family?"

"I said I was going to call," she said.

"Uh-huh."

"I was just…waiting for the right time. That's all."

"You had time to call a television crew, but not your own family? Right. You know, you usually only blow smoke up my butt on Christmas and your birthday, too."

"I'm sorry. There. I said it. Again. I'm the bad guy. Got it. I'll call Mom and Dad and just explain the situation."

"Just explain? You're not going to bring your Hollywood hunk down here to meet the whole family? What? Are you ashamed of us or something?"

"I didn't say that."

"Didn't have to. Your actions speak louder than words—and I have to admit I'm disappointed in you, sis."

"You used to be proud that I escaped from that place," Chloe reminded her. "You used to say that you were going to come live with me when you got old enough."

There was an awkward silence over the line.

"Tess?"

"Corona Mae, it's one thing to leave to go make

something of yourself. It's another thing to act like you've forgotten where you came from."

"I didn't—"

"Look. We've gone around and around on this issue. I get it that you didn't want to be forced into marriage at seventeen. You didn't want to become a teenage house-wife, have a house full of children and work part-time at Momma's hair salon while Lyfe likely joined Daddy at the church and the restaurant. You made your point. But that was a long time ago. Things have changed."

Silence.

"Corona Mae?"

"Yeah. I know. It's not like I don't *ever* call."

"Rarely," Tess corrected.

"It's just that…"

"You're scared of running into *him*," Tess said, as if picking up her sister's thoughts over the line.

"Running into who?" She had no idea why she asked such a stupid question. Tess's bark of laughter was so loud that Chloe had to pull the receiver away from her head in order to save her eardrum.

After a few seconds, she placed the phone back to her ear in time to hear her sister ask, "So are you a talent agent or are you a D-list comedian nowadays?"

"Ha. Ha."

"You damn right, *'ha, ha.'* I mean, really, Corona Mae. Don't treat me like I'm stupid. You might have hauled your butt out of the state and got all your little fancy degrees at all those Ivy-league colleges up there, but I know damn well that you haven't gotten Lyfe Alton out of your system. So play your little Jedi mind trick on someone who doesn't know you."

"I'm sure that Lyfe doesn't spare me a second thought these days. We were just…kids."

"Kids in love. You were each other's first."

"So what? Everybody had a first. It doesn't mean that you walk around pining after them for the rest of your life."

"Please," Tess drawled. "Everyone is still a little in love with their first—especially women. I don't care how awful or how much of a jerk the dude turned out to be, there's still some part of us that's always going to be in love with our first."

"Yeah. Whatever."

"That's the best you got?" Tess laughed. "Pathetic. Why is it so hard for you to admit that you still have feelings for the guy? It's not going to kill you or anything, you know?"

"Because it hurts too much," she finally admitted. "Unless you're telling me that Lyfe personally walked up to you and announced that he still has feelings for me, then I'm just going to assume that since he has never picked up the phone and called me that none of this means anything. I mean—did he even ask about me?"

Silence.

The pain in her chest increased tenfold. "There. You see? Now can we drop it?"

"All right. Fine," Tess finally agreed. "But what about Mel—"

"Drop it!"

"Fine. It's dropped."

"Thank you."

"Well, I better go. Congratulations again on your engagement. Maybe one day you'll tell me about this Rowan James—maybe even introduce him to me."

"Tess—"

"I'll talk to you later. 'Bye."

Chloe was left holding the phone while the dial tone buzzed in her ear. "That went well," she muttered.

Chapter 5

"Yo, Royce. I don't know about this," Lyfe said, climbing out of his F150 truck and then slamming the door behind him. "I really don't feel like hanging out tonight."

His oldest brother Royce waved his whining off his shoulders like a grain of sand. "Spare me. I think Mom or Dad can handle shoveling dog food into Sadie's bowl for one night."

Lyfe hitched up one side of his mouth.

"Seriously, bro." Royce swung his arm around his brother's neck as he led the way toward Henry's Pool Hall. "You need to exchange that bitch for a real woman. I'm starting to worry about you."

"Thanks, but that's not necessary." Lyfe tried to pry himself free from his brother's tight hold, but Royce's thick-muscled arm wasn't having that tonight. He reached and got his older brother into a reverse head-lock and a three-minute wrestling match ensued. It was clearly a draw.

"Whatever happened to that one chick you were seeing a few months back—Kayla, wasn't it? Hennessey said that he thought you were going to finally pop the big question."

"Nah. It was never anything *that* serious." Lyfe chuckled, stretching his neck muscles.

Royce frowned. "You two were together for like two years."

Lyfe's hand stilled on the front door of the pool hall and he tossed his brother an incredulous look. "Wait. You want to give me dating and engagement tips when you've *never* broken your three-month rule?"

Royce shrugged. "And? We're not talking about me. We're talking about you. And *you*—" he jabbed a finger in the center of Lyfe's chest "—aren't like the rest of us. You, unfortunately, inherited that monogamous gene virus that is all the rage with women nowadays."

"You can't be a gene and a virus."

"See." Royce thumped his chest again. "The mere fact that you know that makes you a freak."

Lyfe rolled his eyes again—a habit he had whenever he engaged in these kinds of heart-to-heart talks with his brothers. "Let's just drop it." He jerked open the pool hall's door and was greeted with a thunderous...

"Happy birthday!" everyone in the building shouted, holding up their beer bottles the minute the brothers strolled inside.

Lyfe laughed, then gave everyone a quick two finger salute. "Thanks, everybody. I really appreciate that." He and his brother strolled deeper into the bar toward the back where he knew his other four brothers, Dorian,

Hennessey, Ace and Jacob would be teamed up for their fierce pool competitions.

It was always Dorian and Jacob versus Hennessey and Ace as far back as anyone could remember. Only Royce and Lyfe could either take the game or leave it.

They were all competitive, a trait that had helped both Dorian and Ace to become lawyers and Hennessey to become a music executive. Royce was a farmer like their father, and Jacob worked as an architect in the same firm as Lyfe.

Bragging rights fluctuated from game to game and the obscene amount of money that they would bet was never actually collected by either side. That was true whether it was a game of basketball, football or even, sadly, Monopoly. One thing all the boys had equally mastered was the art of trash talking.

"Well, well. You finally found the runt," Dorian said, sending his custom-made pool stick slamming against the cue ball and causing a thunderous *whack* for the break. "Where did you find him? At home proposing to his main girl, Sadie?"

The Alton brothers laughed.

Ace cut in, "Don't worry. You'll make an honest woman out of that bitch yet."

Lyfe dusted off his shoulders. "Whatever."

"I'm just saying," Ace said.

"One beer for the birthday boy," Leanne announced as she strutted toward him with a single bottle on her tray. "Compliments of the house."

"Why, thank you." He smiled and accepted the gift.

"Annnnnd…" she said, tucking her tray under her arm and producing a blue ribbon and clip.

Lyfe moaned. He hated this part of the tradition. "Aww. Do we have to?"

"C'mon, you know the rules." Leanne winked at him and proceeded to make a bow and pin it to his shirt. "And to get things started, I'm pinning my phone number here first. Now you just make sure that you don't leave me waiting like you did back in high school when you were chasing after Corona Mae."

He smiled at his old high school buddy and senior prom date, who had recently returned to town from Atlanta to help her father run the bar. She had also been a good friend and bridesmaid to Corona Mae. When her friend blew town without a word, she had been hurt as well.

"Hell, if he doesn't call, I most certainly will," Jacob said, assessing her short hemline.

Leanne leveled the charismatic playboy with a withering smile. "No offense, Jacob, but I'd rather put my heart through a meat grinder. It's faster and to the point."

The Alton boys winced at the jab.

"Damn. I guess she told you." Royce laughed, covering his mouth with his fist and shaking his head.

Leanne's no-nonsense gaze shifted to the other brothers, and they all held their breath to see who she was going to take aim at next. "Don't think that just because most of you boys have moved to the big city that everyone has forgotten about your reputations," she warned, waving a finger. "Every woman knows about your ridiculous three-month rule."

The brothers had the good sense to drop their heads and pretend to look busy.

"Uh-huh." Leanne's gaze turned back to the birthday

boy. "Lyfe is the only Alton that's worth a girl getting her hopes up." She winked. "Now you make sure that you call me."

Feeling the spotlight, Lyfe smiled through his wave of embarrassment. At the same time, he felt five distinct holes being burned into his forehead by his glaring brothers.

"I'll be back to bring you another beer when that one gets too low," she informed him with another wink before she sashayed off to take care of her other customers.

"Hey! What about us?" Ace called out, holding up his empty bottle. "We'd like beer, too."

Leanne gave no indication as to whether she'd heard him or not. She just shook her hips as she made her way through the growing crowd.

"It might just be me, but I don't think that she likes us too much," Hennessey concluded.

"Maybe not us, but she clearly loooooves Mr. Romantic here." Ace jutted his thumb at his youngest brother. "It's a good thing that he doesn't visit too often."

Lyfe laughed and thumped on his chest. "What can I say? The woman knows a good thing when she sees it."

His five brothers turned around and pretended to barf all over the floor.

Lyfe opened his mouth to respond, but then a petite beauty in painted-on blue jeans walked up to him smiling. The Alton boys jumped to attention. Dorian attempted to shove Hennessey out of the way, but that was like trying to shove a California Red Oak.

"Well, hello there," Dorian said, leaning against the table and cheesing like the orange cat on a bag of Cheetos. "I know that you're not from around here."

The young woman blushed and revealed a cute set of dimples. "Actually, no. I just moved here," she answered, and then turned her smile toward Lyfe. "The name is Colleen." She reached up and pinned her phone number to his shirt. "Call me." With that, she turned and strolled away.

A full five seconds after she was gone, Jacob held up a finger and squeaked, "I have a phone."

Lyfe sucked in a deep breath to swell up his chest. "Like I said, boys. Women know a good thing when they see it."

For that smartass remark, each brother reached over and whacked him on the back of the skull.

"Hey, yo! Watch the head." Lyfe tried to lean out of reach, but the damage had already been done.

Hennessey frowned. "Why? Ain't nothing in that big noggin.'"

Lyfe patted his freshly low-cut hair and then popped the collar of his tee shirt. "Haters going to hate."

"Yeah, whatever, man," Ace said. "Whose turn is it?"

Jacob cut in, "If you ask me—"

"Nobody asked," Lyfe quipped.

Despite the ensuing chuckle, Jacob continued, "Women flock to your sensitive butt because they recognize that they can train you."

The other brothers nodded in agreement.

"Yeah, you might be a successful architect and making that mad paper, but at the end of the day, you're the kind of brother that will drop everything on a dime to work on women's cars, repair roofs and install things in their houses. Your inner pimp is way the hell out of whack."

Royce bounced his head in agreement. "Not to mention you actually like taking women to those ridiculous chick-flick movies. I don't know how you do that shit. I need a Prozac and a six-pack to get through one of those things."

Lyfe shrugged his broad shoulders. "It's not so bad. You toss your arm around their shoulders and lean them up against your chest during all the romantic parts. What's so hard or bad about that?"

Royce shrugged back. "Nothing, if you don't mind your brain melting out of your head. Me? If I have to sit still for two hours, I prefer to see a lot of bullets, car crashes, and some hot T and A—and not necessarily in that order."

"Amen," the brothers chimed in and lifted up their empty beer bottles in salute.

"Frankly, I don't see what the big deal is," Dorian said. "The women may be slinging their panties at you, but you ain't exactly going to win any catcher of the year awards. I mean, how many girls have you been with since Corona Mae left you standing at the altar? Three…four?"

Lyfe tipped back his bottle as a stall tactic.

"Uh-huh." Dorian shook his head and then aimed to take his next shot. "*That's* a damn shame. What are you waiting on, man? Corona Mae isn't coming back. She's marrying that Tom Cruise wannabe, so now it's time for you to get on with your own life." The cue ball whacked against two of his balls and sent them careening toward the same corner pocket.

Lyfe's grip on his beer bottle tightened, while his other brothers exchanged awkward glances. He couldn't tell whether they thought that Dorian was being too blunt or were relieved that he had said what they had all been thinking. All he knew was that the heat blazing up his neck wasn't embarrassment. "I'm *not* waiting for her to return," he growled. Whether the statement was the truth or not wasn't something that he wanted to analyze right now.

Still hunched over the pool table, Dorian glanced up. "Are you sure?"

"Hello, excuse me?"

Lyfe turned to see Ashlee, the new checkout girl at the Piggly Wiggly, who his mother had spent considerable time trying to introduce him to. She smiled up at him as she pinned her number to his chest.

"This is for you, birthday boy. You make sure that you call me." With a wink, she turned and walked away.

"Hmph! Hmph! Hmph! I definitely think that her ass is asking a question," Jacob said, referring to how her butt was shaped like an upside down question mark. "How about I play you for her number?"

Lyfe shook his head.

"Why? We all know that you're not going to call her."

"Give it a rest," Lyfe warned. Being the youngest, he was used to being picked on and harassed; but tonight he really wasn't in the mood. For two days, he'd been doing everything he could to get that damn interview out of his head. But nothing was working.

Corona Mae, or Chloe as she was calling herself nowadays, was getting married. No big deal. He was happy for her. He should be happy. He would be happy—eventually—as soon as Leanne brought him enough beers to get a good buzz going.

They claimed a nearby table and stool and ordered hot wings and fries. Royce announced that he and Lyfe would play the winner in the next game. For the next hour, Lyfe watched the game without seeing, listened to his brothers' jokes without hearing, and drank his beer without tasting it. All that played in his head was the image of Corona Mae smiling at Hollywood's most bankable star like she had finally found *The One*.

He tipped up his fourth drink, hoping that this bottle would be the one to dull the persistent and growing ache in the center of his chest. It didn't.

Corona had definitely developed into quite a looker. She was no longer the seventeen-year-old teenager en-grained in his memory. For years he wondered what he would say or do if their paths ever crossed again. Four-teen years later, he still didn't have an answer. It looked like he really didn't need one either. They lived in two different worlds.

"C'mon. You're going to have to try to cheer up," Jacob said, walking over to Lyfe. "This is supposed to be a birthday party, remember?"

"Oh, yeah? So where are my gifts?" Lyfe challenged.

The brother's started whistling and looking all around like bees were buzzing about their heads.

"Cheap bastards," Lyfe mumbled.

Suddenly they all broke out into smiles and guffaws. Dorian stepped forward and looped his arm around Lyfe's neck. "I have a gift for you."

The cocksure smile that covered his brother's face made Lyfe curious and suspicious.

"Since you seem to have it for a Banks girl. Maybe all this time, you've just been looking at the wrong one?"

"What?"

Dorian grabbed him by the shoulders and spun him

around toward the front door as Tess Banks strolled into the place, looking like a million bucks and waaaay too much like her sister.

Chapter 6

November 30. Lyfe's birthday.

After all these years, Corona had never forgotten the date. It had become a private tradition for her to stop and wonder what Lyfe was doing, who he was seeing and whether he was happy. And, more importantly, whether he had found it in his heart to forgive her. While riding in the back of a Maybach, Corona removed her reading glasses and stared out of the tinted windows. In the years since she had transplanted to New York, she had never really gotten used to the fast pace of the concrete jungle. She didn't know how anyone really got used to it. People were always in a rush to get to God knows where, and there was rarely a smile to be seen anywhere.

It was a far cry from Thomason, where everybody knew everyone else's business. Smiles were given out like Halloween candy; and if you stood still, you'd swear you could hear the grass growing in everyone's front yard.

Corona closed her eyes, and a memory of home materialized. She remembered how every Monday the scent of fresh baked bread would fill the entire house. Tuesday it would be the pie of the week that would get most of the family in trouble when they tried to sneak slices before dinner. Wednesday it would be some mouthwatering cake that would always be handed out after Bible study. Baking wasn't her mother's only talent. From pot roast to collard greens, her mother was a master in the kitchen.

Tugging in a deep breath, Corona was almost certain that she could smell her momma's cooking right now. So much so, that she almost clicked her heels three times. How could a place so far away suddenly seemed so close?

An image of seventeen-year-old Lyfe tugging on his oversized tuxedo surfaced and guilt's spidery fingers crept up her spine and then settled on her shoulders. She wasn't supposed to see him before the wedding, but her nerves were so knotted together that she thought if she just snuck a peek, it would calm her down.

It hadn't.

Corona slipped on her reading glasses and turned another page.

December 23, 1998
Dear Diary,
It's been a week since my parents walked in on me and Lyfe. And so much is changing so fast. Just this morning, I was standing in the middle of my bedroom, staring at my reflection while Momma

carefully looped what seemed like the millionth pearl button on the back of her old wedding gown.

"Oh, just look at you." Momma sighed. "My dress fits you perfectly."

Did it? I thought the virginal white gown was cutting off my air supply.

Not to mention, it felt like it weighed a ton.

"C'mon, sweetheart. There's no reason to make such a long face. Everything is going to be fine. You'll see."

"Fine?" *I twisted around to stare at her incredulously.* "It's a shotgun wedding. Daddy is forcing us to get married!"

"Lower your voice," *Momma commanded with a pinched face.* "My goodness. I'm not deaf."

"Well, we have to do something, Momma. This isn't the seventeenth century. I don't have to get married just because I'm not a virgin anymore."

She flinched and, for a second, the same look of disappointment that had seized Daddy's face these past six days flickered across her face.

I gasped and then twisted back around toward the mirror, this time with tears glossing my eyes.

"Now, sweetheart," *Momma tried again.* "Your father is just doing what he thinks is right in this situation. He's a preacher in this town and—"

"So I have to get married in order to save his reputation, is that it? I got to tell you, Mom. That's pretty jacked up."

"Stop it," *she snapped and then took a step back.* "I won't have you talk about your father in that tone of voice. You will show and give him the proper respect." *Momma took a couple of deep breaths before her face and voice softened. "Look, baby. You know that we love you and that we're just doing what we feel is best for you."*

I pressed my lips together, but it didn't stop them from trembling. In the mirror I saw that my response just added stress lines to Momma's face.

"I don't understand," Momma said, shaking her head. "I thought that you loved Lyfe."

"I do," I answered instantly. "It's just that... this is all happening so fast."

"Sort of how things just happened last week?"

I didn't like having my weak explanation of what happened between me and Lyfe being tossed back at me like that. I'd broken the golden rule about not having boys in the house when my parents weren't home. In truth, we'd been breaking that rule a hell of a lot more since the beginning of our senior year. Suddenly we had new emotions and hormones that were just raging out of control.

My parents had to have sensed it. They were always trying to talk to me about the birds and the bees.

Daddy took to the task literally and got lost in breaking down the whole bee and flower pollination explanation. It ended up being the longest two hour talk of my entire life.

"Corona Mae," Momma said, tilting up my chin. "Don't you want to marry him?"

"I...do," I answered softly.

Finally a smile exploded across Momma's face. "You love him and you want to marry him—so what's the problem?"

"I...I..."

"*It's just wedding jitters,*" *she diagnosed proudly.* "*You'll be fine once you become Mrs. Lyfe Alton.*" *Momma winked.* "*Now wait right here. I want to give you something.*" *With that, she turned and rushed out of the bedroom.*

"*Mrs. Lyfe Alton,*" *I repeated, staring at my reflection.*

Tess spoke up, "*You don't look so good, Mrs. Alton.*"

I cut a look across the room to where my ten-year-old sister sat, looking annoyed for having been forced into a dress when it wasn't a Sunday. But then I realized that I needed an ally. "*Tess, I need for you to do me a favor.*"

"*It'll cost you five dollars,*" *Tess said, jutting out a hand.*

"*I haven't even told you what it is yet,*" *I complained.*

"*Doesn't matter. Five dollars.*"

I stared her down.

"*You want to make it ten?*"

"*Fine. Five dollars.*" *I yanked up my yards of fabric and stormed over to my top chest of drawers.* "*Turn around,*" *I commanded.*

Tess huffed but quickly did as I told her.

Once I was sure that my sister wasn't peeking, I kneeled and reached for the loose plank beside the drawers and withdrew my stash of saved allowance. I moved quickly and came up with the five dollars to bribe my sister.

"*Here.*"

Tess turned back around and greedily snatched

*the money from my hand. "All right. What can I
do for you?"*

*"Go find Lyfe and tell him to come and meet
me in the basement."*

*"Corona Mae, it's bad luck for you to see the
groom before the wedding," Tess warned as she
tried to pull me back toward her bedroom.*

*"Please spare me all those foolish old wives'
tales," I said, gathering up the yards of lace so
that I could move faster. I had to hurry before
Momma returned to fulfill her promise to give
me something old, something new and something
blue.*

*All I knew at that moment was that everything
was just moving so fast. The beautiful moment that
me and Lyfe had shared before my parents had
busted in now had me barreling toward one of the
fastest shotgun marriages in history. Seven days.
I really hadn't had much time to digest everything
that was happening, so I could only imagine what
Lyfe must be feeling.*

*There was a huge difference between wanting
to sleep with your girlfriend and having to marry
her. But by the time Daddy got through preach-
ing fire and brimstones, I had an engagement ring
and a wedding date.*

*I hadn't even seen him, let alone talked to him,
since he ran out my parents' house naked. Of
course I hadn't been able to do much talking to
my father either. There had been a lot of shouting
and ordering me around, but no talking. Momma
assured me that things would work themselves out*

after the wedding and that Daddy was just hurt and disappointed.

I never meant to hurt him—or anyone for that matter. There was a lot going on with me. My body. My emotions. It was all just so complicated.

"You're making a mistake," Tess continued, rushing behind me in her best Sunday dress.

"Yeah. Yeah. Whatever. Just do me this one favor," I said, reaching the side door.

Tess rolled her eyes and settled her hands on her pencil-thin hips. "Sure, Batman. I'll jump right on it."

I placed my hands on my sister's shoulders and looked her in the eye. "Tell him it's important."

"And how is he going to meet you there? Daddy is watching him like a hawk in case he's thinking about bolting."

"Please. Just do it," I begged. "Lyfe will figure something out." I turned my sister around by her shoulders and then scooted her out the back door with a reverent prayer.

Ten minutes later, I had damn near paced a hole into the basement's concrete flooring. Did Tess deliver the message? Was he coming? Hell, I wasn't even sure what I was going to say, let alone how I was going to say it. Maybe when I saw him, it would all come to me. I just knew it.

"Corona Mae?"

I jerked at the sound of Lyfe's low whisper. Suddenly, my heart felt as if it was trying to escape through my throat.

"Corona, are you down here?"

"Over here," I croaked.

Lyfe crept down the darkened staircase and looked around. The moment his eyes landed on me, he froze. "My God." His gaze slowly caressed me from head to toe. "You look beautiful."

I flushed. Until that moment, I had thought I was drowning in a sea of fabric. But now, seeing his reaction, I started to feel beautiful. "Thanks." I whispered and then took a moment to assess him. His tall frame filled out his tuxedo rather nicely. With broad shoulders, a toned body, and still a bit of a baby face, I knew that Lyfe was on the cusp of being GQ fine, just like the other men in his family.

But if I was forced to pick my favorite feature, it would definitely be his eyes. His dark, soul-searing eyes were always filled with such love and honesty. There were times when he would just look at me and I would melt like a snowball being hurled toward the sun.

He walked down the rest of the staircase and made a beeline toward me. "Uhm. Should we be meeting like this before the wedding? I thought it was considered bad luck?"

For the second time, I waved off that foolishness. "I wanted...needed to talk to you." I clasped my hands together and started wringing my fingers. "I wanted to see where your head was at with all of this." I locked eyes with him. "You know, with my father forcing you to marry me."

Lyfe opened his mouth, but then quickly closed it.

My brain seized on his hesitation as confir-

mation that he was also having second thoughts. "You don't want to do this," I concluded.

"No. No. I didn't say that," he said, quickly trying to cover his initial reaction. He even grabbed my tangled hands.

"We don't have to go through with it," I said. "I doubt that my father will really shoot you if we don't get married."

"Ha! You're talking to a guy who had bullets whizzing by his ass just a few nights ago. He'll shoot. Believe me...and the next time he won't miss." He laughed.

But did he want to get married? That was the question that I was having trouble getting past my lips. What if he didn't, but said that he did— or worse, said that he did and meant it.

My mother's dress was slowly suffocating me. I pulled my hands back and then pressed them against my nervous stomach. This was all my father's doing. It had nothing to do with how we felt about each other or whether this was the right thing to do. It had everything to do with his "hurt and disappointment." Hell, I didn't even know what I wanted. What about school and college or getting a job and finding our own place? Seventeen was too young to get married, wasn't it?

"Corona?" Lyfe took hold of my hands and then brought them up to his lips. "Are you all right? Is something troubling you?"

"Well...it's..." I looked back up into his inquiring eyes and my tongue began to swell up in my throat. If we went through with this, it could

possibly ruin his life—ruin both our lives. "It's just...you know...wedding jitters. You know?"

Lyfe nodded and then drew me into his arms. "It's going to be alright. It's not like getting married is the worst thing in the world. We've been together for a long time now, right?"

"Right." That was hardly the most romantic thing a man could say on his wedding day. But what did I expect when he hadn't technically proposed? My father produced a gun, Lyfe came up with a ring, and now here we were.

The basement door crept open and I nearly jumped out my skin. Had my father found us? Was he about to march us back upstairs with our hands up in the air?

Tess poked her head inside. "Y'all better come on. People are starting to look for you. Momma is trying to keep Daddy from his rifle cabinet."

Lyfe's eyes bulged. "We better go!"

"Oh...all right then," I said, disappointed. My stomach looped into sailor's knots. In a few minutes, we were going to be married.

Before racing to the door, Lyfe smiled and brushed a kiss against my upturned face. "I'll meet you at the altar," he whispered.

I tried not to drown in his cognac gaze, but it was hard. I did love him—had loved him for as long as I could remember. Instinctively, I reached out and cupped the side of his face. "I love you."

A smile exploded across Lyfe's face. "I love you, too," he said and stole another kiss. "Always have...always will."

"Oh, brother. Get a room." Tess rolled her eyes.

"There you two are." Royce Alton poked his head in above Tess. "Do you know that the whole wedding party has been out here looking for you two?"

"Hey, what's going on?" Hennessey's head joined the stack of heads that were peering past the door. "What are y'all doing down here?"

Lyfe heaved out a long, frustrated breath. "Damn, y'all. We were just talking."

"Before the wedding?" Hennessey asked. "Isn't that considered bad luck or something?"

Tess bobbed her head. "Yep. I told her that."

"We're coming. We're coming," I snapped. Our moment of privacy was officially over.

"Better hurry up," Royce said. "I heard Mr. Banks on the phone talking to the sheriff about blocking the main road out of town."

"You got to be kidding me," I said, but I had no doubts that my father would do just that.

"I better go," Lyfe told me, but instead of heading toward the door, he cocked his head. "Are you sure that you're all right?"

It was now or never.

"I...I...I."

"Lyfe! Corona," Daddy thundered from somewhere in the house.

"Guys!" Tess huffed with another roll of her eyes. "Everybody is waiting."

"I better go." Lyfe delivered another peck to the side of my cheek and then finally took off toward the garage door, where he disappeared with his brothers.

The minute the boys were gone, my shoulders drooped with the weight of the world.

Tess lingered at the door. "Corona?"

"Uhhh...oh. I'm coming."

"But—"

"Please," I begged, close to tears. "Just stall Momma for a few more minutes."

Tess stared, but then finally nodded and ran off.

I sucked in a deep breath, but for some reason I still couldn't breathe. I tried again and then again, until I was chugging in so much air that I was hyperventilating. I couldn't do this. I wouldn't do this—not to Lyfe or to myself. There was so much I wanted to do before I could even consider getting married. And I knew that there were things that Lyfe wanted to do as well.

It was one of those times when if you truly love someone, you have to set them free.

Resolute, I gathered up the yards of silk and rushed back up the staircase, then blew into my bedroom like a hurricane. Two seconds later, my sister rushed in. "Help me out of this thing," I ordered.

"What?"

"You heard me. The job pays twenty dollars."

That got my sister to move. In no time, Tess had unfastened the pearl buttons on the back of my dress, and then I ordered her to lock the door and help me pack.

"But where are you going?" Tess asked, nervously. "Hennessey wasn't kidding. Daddy asked Sheriff Cooper to block the main roads."

"Then I'll take the back roads," I said, grabbing my small suitcases out of the closet.

Tess blinked. *"You're running away?"*

"I have to. This isn't right and Daddy isn't listening to reason," I huffed as I pulled clothes out of my drawers and started cramming them into my suitcases. *"This is my life, and I'm going to make my own decisions."*

"But...but..."

"All I need is a head start."

"But where?"

"I'm going to stay with Aunt Charlene."

"In New York? How are you going to get all the way up there?"

I dropped to my knees beside the chest of drawers and quickly pulled out my stash. Being a sought-after babysitter in town, I had managed to save a lot of my money. All I needed to do was borrow my father's car to the airport and my cash would take care of the rest.

"I don't know about this," Tess said, backing toward the bedroom door.

I caught the sneaky movement out of the corner of my eye, and I flew to the door and locked it before my sister had a chance to bolt. *"Snitches get stitches,"* I warned with a wave of my finger.

Tess gulped as her eyes widened.

Unless I wanted to tie my sister to a chair, I would need to go at this another way. *"I'm sorry. I don't mean to scare you...it's just that I can't marry Lyfe right now. It isn't right. You know it. We all know it. And if I don't stop this train wreck, I'm going to regret it for the rest of my life."*

"But I thought that you loved him."

"I do. And I will always love him. But getting married like this...at our age, is going to destroy our love before it ever has a real chance of getting off the ground. We need to have a chance to grow into ourselves before we try to blend our lives together. I want to finish high school. Go to college. Start a career. And I know that he wants those things too." Tears blurred my vision as I cocked my head and stared into my sister's eyes. "Don't you understand?"

Tess hesitated, but then she slowly nodded.

"Good. So you'll help me?"

"All right."

I drew my sister into my arms. "Thank you. Thank you so much." When I stood back up, I wiped at my eyes and dove back into my packing. When I finally got my two bags stuffed with all I was ever going to get into them, I headed toward my bedroom window.

Tess stopped me. "Wait. What about Lyfe? Shouldn't you leave him a note or something?"

I blinked. "I don't know what to say."

"You need to say something."

"I...I can't."

"But—"

"What can I say that won't make him come chasing after me? If I apologize and tell him that I still love him, then he'll come after me. You know he will...or he'll just sit here and wait until I come back. I don't want him to do that."

"But if you just disappear, it will break his heart—and what about Mom and Dad?"

More tears rushed to my eyes. *"If I break his heart, then he won't come after me and try to change my mind. And I'm not so sure that he wouldn't be able to change my mind if he tried. And Mom and Dad...I'll call them when I get there."*

"But—"

"No. This is best," I decided firmly. *"No note."*

Tess just pressed her lips together. *"You'll call me once you get there, won't you?"*

"Of course I will." I smiled.

The bedroom door knob jiggled, and then there was a knock.

"Corona Mae, are you in there?"

Tess's eyes bulged.

"Yes, Momma. I'll be right out." I turned toward my sister again. *"Give me five minutes before you let her in."*

"They're going to kill me you know," Tess complained.

"I really appreciate you doing this for me."

"Yeah. Sure. Whatever."

I delivered a quick peck to her plump cheek. *"I love you, lil' T. I'll call you as soon as I get to Aunt Charlene's."* With that I ducked out of the window and raced away from my wedding, determined not to look back...

"We're here, Ms. Banks," the driver announced.

Corona snapped out of the past and closed her diary. However, her chest still ached as if she'd just made that heart-wrenching decision a few seconds ago. After all this time, there were still so many *"what-ifs"* tumbling around her head like Texas tumbleweed.

The driver opened the back door and Corona glanced up as ten-year-old Melody climbed into the car and smiled at her with her father's cognac gaze.

"Hey, Mom."

Chapter 7

"Well, well. Lookie here. It's the birthday boy!" Tess stepped in front of Lyfe and crowded his personal space. Her bright brown eyes and apple-cheeked smile was like a punch in the gut. Lyfe had to take a deep breath and lean back from her in order to get his bearings.

"It's the second time in three days that we've run into each other. We better watch out, this could actually mean something." Tess laughed and reached up to pin her number to his chest. "Here you go, handsome."

He glanced down and shook his head. "Uh, I don't think that is such a hot idea."

When he started to unpin the number, she covered his hand with her own. "Don't be so hasty. You know there *is* a chance that you were just with the wrong Banks girl." She shifted her brows up. "If you get my drift."

His brothers exchanged knowing looks and cocky smiles.

Lyfe's laugh was out of his mouth before he had a chance to consider whether it would hurt her feelings. He didn't have to look over at the pool table to know that he was once again the center of attention.

Tess's brows stretched up.

"No offense, Tess, but I can't help but look at you like a little sister."

Hennessey leaned over to remind him, "We don't have a sister."

"And if we had one that looked like her, I'd gouge my eyes out," Dorian said, as his gaze slowly caressed her curves.

The glowing comments made Tess toss them each a devastating smile. "Why thank you, guys. You always did know how to say the nicest things—though I wouldn't date a single one of you."

The brothers snickered.

"So Thanksgiving is over with… You thinking about hanging around?" Tess asked.

"Can't say that I am—though I do miss it around here," Lyfe said. It was the truth. He loved the simple life and the friendly people. People in the city moved too fast for him, and they never seemed to really take the time to notice things around them. Was it so wrong to like coming home to a house that wasn't inches from the neighbors? Hell, who could tell all those suburban McMansions from one another anyway?

The urban world was just a place where everyone killed themselves trying to keep up with Joneses. They all had to have the same houses, the same cars, and damn near the same trophy wives and two point five children. It was insane—and yet, there he was, participating in the rat race, trying to prove to the memory of a seventeen-year-old Corona that he had what it took to be successful in the big cities, too.

He would never admit that truth to anyone, not even himself.

But since he'd been back, he'd been having some odd dreams; one with him living in a nice house with a huge yard and a wraparound porch. He could picture himself, sitting on a porch swing in the evenings with Sadie at his side, listening to crickets and watching the sun go down. A couple of times, he dreamed that Corona Mae would one day join him out on that porch. Maybe in the yard there would be a dozen mini-me's running around, filling the evening sky with the sounds of their exuberant laughter.

Silly him.

Tess cocked her head and then waved her hand in front of his face. "Hello. Earth to Lyfe. Is anyone home?"

"Huh? What?"

Tess's eyes narrowed suspiciously. "And who are you thinking about?"

With perfect timing, Leanne popped up and set another bottle down. "You're hitting these pretty hard tonight."

"I can't imagine why," he mumbled under his breath.

Tess smiled. "Maybe because you have someone on your mind? I don't know. Maybe someone who's getting married soon?"

Lyfe rolled his eyes and reached for his new drink. Had everyone taken up pouring salt in people's wounds as a hobby?

"Maybe someone you should call?" She tugged his ribbon. "Hint—that's not *my* number."

Lyfe took another look at the number and for the first time noticed the 917 area code. "New York?"

"Yea." Tess clapped her hands. "Everyone give him a round of applause."

His brothers, always up for embarrassing and humiliating him, gave her the resounding applause she was looking for.

"Why are you giving me a New York number?" Then it hit him. "Oh."

Tess twisted up her face. "You know, I think I gave you more points for intelligence than you're due."

"A lot of people make that mistake." Royce chuckled.

Lyfe tried to remove the number pinned to his chest. "In that case, I still don't think that I need—"

"Of course you do. Corona Mae is getting married... or have you forgotten?"

"Well, good for her," he said, turning up his bottle again.

Tess laughed in his face. "You two really are pathetic."

Suspicious, Lyfe lowered his beer and eyed her wearily. "Two?"

"You're not just going to let her marry that guy, are you?"

"Let her?" He laughed. "I don't believe I have any say in the matter."

This time Tess cocked her head and jammed her hands onto her hips. "Wow. Waaaay more points than you deserve."

Lyfe set his bottle down. Clearly he'd already had too many if he was having a hard time following this conversation. "What are you getting at, Tess?"

"Look, Lyfe, let me give it to you straight. Everyone

in this town knows that you still have the hots for my sister." She glanced around and asked, "Am I right?"

The crowd, all the way up to the bar, yelled back, "Yeah!"

Tess turned back around. "See? Don't get me wrong, you've been doing an admirable job trying not to show it, but you're not fooling anyone. I saw how you watched that interview the other day. Admit it."

Lyfe was a second away from denying the charge, but stopped short when he saw his brothers lined up by the pool table, ready to call him on his bullshit. "Look. Maybe you all forgot, but *I* was all set to marry Corona Mae a decade ago. She's the one that left *me*. I emptied out my measly savings account and bought her a diamond. And I was left standing in a too-small rented tuxedo with half the town staring at me."

"Diamond chip," Tess corrected for another round of chuckles. "A hundred and fifty bucks don't get you far, even if it was back in the day."

"Whatever! I was proud of that ring." He sat up straighter. "It was the best I could afford."

"There was always the bubble gum machine," Dorian said, jumping in on the act. "Who knows, if you'd gotten her a ring from there, she might've showed up."

"All right, enough," Lyfe barked. Everyone jumped at his harsh tone, and he realized that maybe he needed to call it a night and just get back home to Sadie. "Look, guys, I'm really not up to this. I think that I should go."

"Fine. I'll drive you home," Tess said, snatching his keys off the table.

"To Atlanta?"

"You've been drinking."

"I also have five brothers here who can drive me home."

"Home? I'm not ready to go home," Royce said, glancing around. "Anybody ready to go home?"

Like good little soldiers, the rest of the Alton clan shook their heads and pretended like they couldn't possibly be torn away from the party of the century.

"Good. Then it's settled. I'll drive you." Tess smiled broadly.

Lyfe glowered at his brothers. "Judases."

"C'mon, Lyfe. I'm just trying to help you do what you should've done a long time ago—get your girlfriend back."

When his face twisted in confusion, she added, "I'll explain my plan on the drive home. And then you can thank me later."

Chapter 8

"I thought you said that this was just going to be a small intimate party," Corona said, settling down into her vanity chair to put the final touches on her make-up.

"According to my mother, a hundred of her closest friends qualifies as a small party." Rowan chuckled as he fidgeted with his tie. "If you're going to be a part of the James clan you better get used to these sorts of things."

"Warning received," Corona mumbled and then took a deep breath. "It just seems like we're always going to one party or another. It would be nice if we could just carve out some quality time with Melody."

Rowan's hands fell to his sides. "You think that's going to help her warm up to me?"

Corona shrugged and held on to her optimism. "At the very least it will help her get used to the idea of our getting married."

"Wishful thinking." He laughed then began attempting round two with his tie. "If that's what you think, then I have a bridge in Brooklyn that I can sell you."

She laughed. "C'mon. It's not that bad."

"Oh? Is that why she told me that she thought that people who made a living by pretending to be other people were stupid?"

Shocked, Corona dropped her blush brush and jerked around on her small chair. "She did not!"

"Oh, she most certainly did," he said, laughing and shaking his head. "That was about a minute before she said that she didn't know how she felt about having a *white* father."

Corona's mouth stretched wider.

Rowan turned away from the full-length mirror with his tie perfectly aligned. "It's okay. I know that she's just acting out. It's been the two of you for so long, so now she doesn't want to share. I get it."

"That's still no excuse," she said, finally finding her voice. Melody was certainly a beautiful child, but Corona wasn't blind to the fact that her child was a handful. "Tomorrow when she comes back from her sleepover, we're going to have a looong talk."

Rowan shook his head. "Nah. Don't do that."

"But—"

"I have to win her over on my own," he said, strolling across the spacious bedroom and settling his hands on her shoulder. "If you go running off and reprimanding her every time we talk, then she's going to stop talking to me all together."

"But—"

"Trust me on this." Rowan tilted up her chin. "I used to pull this same stunt on every one of my stepmothers."

Corona lifted a brow. "You chased them all away?"

"Nah. My father's habitual cheating took care of that. I just didn't see the point in being nice to them if they weren't going to stick around."

"Is that supposed to reassure me?"

"Yes." He leaned down and brushed a kiss against her lips. "Once Melody sees that I'm not going anywhere, then she'll open up."

It made sense, but Corona remained dubious.

"Trust me," he repeated.

"All right." She shrugged. "My lips are sealed—but you *will* tell me if she says something that's really out of line, right?"

He held up his hands. "Scout's honor."

Corona cocked her head as she narrowed her eyes.

"All right. I was never a scout, but I did play one on TV once." He winked.

"Ha. Ha." She stood and headed over to her jewelry chest. While she picked out a pair of loop diamond earrings, her gaze settled on the small golden band with a tiny diamond chip in the center, and suddenly she felt a tightening in her chest. She reached and brushed her finger over the ring, but didn't pick it up.

"Medlody will be fine," Rowan said, coming up behind her. "Trust me on this."

"I didn't say—"

"You didn't have to." He brushed a kiss against the back of her shoulder. "It's written all over your face."

Corona drew a deep breath. "You know me so well."

"I'd like to think I do."

She turned around and allowed him to pull her into his arms. "What is that supposed to mean?"

"Well…usually by the time a man proposes to a

woman," he began, peppering her nose with kisses, "he has met his future in-laws."

Corona tensed and tried to pull out of his arms. "I... just...I don't know if—"

"All right." He held up his hands. "I didn't mean to stress you out or anything. Let's just calm down and try to have a good time tonight. You think that we can do that?"

Corona chugged in another deep breath and nodded.

"Then can I at least get a smile?" He tilted his head and waited until her lips thinned out into a smile. "That's my girl." He swiped another kiss on her lips and then gave her a loving smack on the ass. "We better hurry. We don't want to be late to our own party."

Ask him, she urged herself. "Uh...Rowan, there's something that I've been meaning to ask you."

"Oh?" He reached for his evening jacket.

"Yeah." She tried to force casualness into her voice. "You didn't happen to have stumbled on to any of my... books in the walk-in closet, have you?"

He turned with a raised brow. "You read while you're in your closet?"

"No...no. I don't read in there. It just happens to be where I store some of my personal things."

His confusion deepened.

"Oh, never mind," she said, convinced that he didn't have a clue what she was talking about. "It's not a big deal." Maybe she had just imagined that her secret hide-away had been tampered with.

Rowan walked over and wrapped his arms around her again. "Did you lose a book or something?"

"No. It's just... Please forget about it. Let's just get to this damn party so this evening can be over with."

Rowan lifted a brow. "An interesting way to view our engagement party."

"Nooo. I didn't mean it like that." Why did she keep putting her foot in her mouth? "Really, baby." She lifted up on her toes and delivered a quick kiss. "I'm excited about the party."

"And the wedding?"

She swallowed and had trouble pushing up a smile. "And the wedding."

An hour later, Corona and Rowan smiled and mingled through a swarm of guests offering them congratulations and well-wishes. Since it was the holidays, the decor was a combination of white Christmas and romantic soft pinks. It was a rare event when she was the center of attention in a room of so many celebrities and industry elite. Usually, she was promoting a client, not herself. Nights like tonight reminded her why she liked being behind the scenes. The whole process was exhausting and overwhelming. It was nothing like things were back home, where there was just a natural ease in talking to people you'd known your entire life.

She frowned at that last rogue thought. How many times have she been thinking about home lately?

"You two must be sooo happy," Danica Foxx said, appearing out of nowhere.

Corona blinked, surprised to see her fiancé's ex at *her* engagement party. "As a matter of fact, we are." She tightened her hold around Rowan's waist for support.

"Good." Danica's lips thinned into a flat line. "After all, it's all I've ever wanted for Rowan—for him to be happy."

"You could've fooled me," Rowan snickered, then lifted his drink and downed the contents in one gulp.

The woman's red lips smiled, but her faux mink lashes blinked one time too many.

Back off, bitch, Corona tried to convey the message telepathically through her own narrowed gaze. "Excuse me, but what in the hell are you doing here?" she asked with her old southern-charm voice.

"Oh, I guess Wahida didn't tell you?"

"Tell me what?" Corona asked.

"Oh, there you are, dahhling," Wahida James cooed. She plowed through her guests like a Mack truck and didn't bother to see how many bodies she left in her wake. "I thought that you would never get here."

Danica turned with a bright Hollywood smile and greeted the woman with a dramatic embrace and an exchange of air kisses. "Of course I made it. Who could say no to one of your fabulous parties?"

"How about when you're not welcomed at one?" Corona challenged.

Wahida pretended to be offended. "Why, Chloe, where are your manners? Danica is a close friend of the family. I only invited her because I knew that she didn't hold any ill-feeling just because things didn't work out between her and Rowan."

Danica bobbed her head, but the smile on her face resembled a Cheshire cat. "Absolutely. I didn't mean to offend or upset you. I thought that since Rowan and I will be working together in London next week that everything was good between us."

"What?" Corona turned toward her fiancé. "You didn't tell me that she was in the movie."

Danica laughed while Rowan tried to take another gulp of his drink, only to be reminded that it was empty.

"Ah. Ah. Ah. Looks like someone is back to his bad boy ways," said Danica.

Rowan cleared his throat. "Didn't I? Maybe I just assumed you knew since it had made the trade papers."

"You assumed?" Corona repeated, feeling heat rush up her neck and face.

"I, uhm…" Rowan finally caught sight of a passing waiter and launched at him like a NASA rocket, trying to get at another drink.

Left standing alone in front of Wahida and Danica, Corona sucked in a deep breath. "Well, at any rate, I find extending an invitation to an ex-girlfriend highly inappropriate, Wahida. In the future I'd appreciate it if you'd check with me before inviting any more of Rowan's ex-girlfriends to parties that we're attending."

Without missing a beat, Wahida shrugged. "If you're trying to avoid women that my son has slept with in this city, or in any other town, then you're going to leave me with hardly anyone to invite."

"Ain't that the truth." Danica snickered.

Great. These two heifers were a tag team. "Whatever, I need some air." Corona turned and plowed through the people who were standing behind her. She just happened to be by the door when she heard a loud knock. "Good Lord. More people?" She glanced around Rowan's apartment and wondered where they were to put more people.

Dismissing the urge to march past it, she stopped, downed the rest of her drink and then painted on a smile. But when she opened the door, the smile melted right off as her gaze crashed into her mother.

"Mom."

"Hello, dear," her mother greeted nervously as she pulled another body in front of the door.

"Daddy?" Corona's champagne glass slipped from her hand and crashed to the floor.

Chapter 9

"Hello, Corona Mae," her father said, flatly.

The hair on the back of Corona's neck jumped to attention at the sound of her father saying her name. Her heart, which was rolling around in her Prada shoes, started pounding in double time.

Despite the full graying of his hair, the hard grooved lines in his forehead and the even smaller lines around his eyes, he looked the same. Before she could contain it, a swell of love poured from her heart while her vision blurred with a rush of tears.

Standing next to him, her mother was smiling with her own streams of tears pouring down her face. "Our baby," she whispered, clutching her husband's arms. "Rufus, look at her. Doesn't she look beautiful?"

He nodded while his Adam's apple bobbed fiercely in his throat. "She's a dead ringer for her mother." Slowly, he opened his arms. "I hope it's not too much to ask for a hug…"

Corona stood there blinking like an idiot. When she realized that everyone was looking at her, she pushed on a smile, but the damn thing refused to stay up. When she tried to get her legs to move forward, there seemed to be a short circuit somewhere between her brain and her muscles.

"Chloe?" Rowan said, moving to her side. "Are you all right, sweetheart?"

"That wasn't exactly the response I was looking for." Her father chuckled awkwardly.

If they were waiting for her to fill the void, they were going to be waiting a long time, because Corona was convinced that her drink had been spiked and she was seeing things. That was the only explanation for what she was seeing.

Her father's arms started to close, and her parents' smiles faltered.

Rowan spoke up. "Honey, who do we have here?" He turned on his box office smile while he waited for an answer.

"Uhm, sweetheart, this is uhm, my…parents."

"You're kidding." Rowan's face fell, but in the next second he regained his composure. "Well, welcome! C'mon in," he said, enthusiastically seizing her father's hand and working it like an old water pump. "Oh, Mr. Banks, I can't tell you what a pleasure it is to finally meet you."

"Uh…same here." Her father guffawed and seemed concerned that the famous actor was trying to unhinge his arm.

"I can't believe this," Rowan said. "Chloe and I were

just talking about my meeting her family—and here you are." He finally released her father's arm.

Her father's gaze shifted over to her. "Chloe," he repeated, twisting his face. "Is that what you're calling yourself now? I thought that was just a typo on the invitation."

Corona blinked at him. "Invitation?"

Rowan released her father's hand to turn toward her mother. "Mrs. Banks," Rowan said, stretching his arms wide. "Now I see where my fiancée gets her looks. I swear that you can pass as her twin sister."

Adele Banks's entire face flushed a deep burgundy as Rowan swept her into his arms to give her a big bear hug. Of course, the tears hadn't stopped streaking down her face since the moment Corona had opened the door, and they had ruined her makeup.

"What happened here?" Rowan looked down at the shattered glass he was stepping on.

Corona cleared her throat. "I, uhm—dropped my glass."

"She was just so surprised to see *us*," her mother said.

"Well, she's not the only one," Rowan said and then signaled for someone to come clean up the glass. "I know someone else that will be pleased to meet you, too."

He looked around the room and Corona's heart squeezed inside her chest. "Rowan, sweetheart, you don't have to—"

"Mother," he shouted just a decibel above the chattering crowd and the tinkling Christmas tunes coming from the piano player. "Mother, come here for a moment."

Wahida's head popped up like a weasel and, before

Corona could do anything about it, the woman was plowing back through the crowd, ignoring the many feet and ankles she tramped on. "Yes, dear? What is it?" She shifted her cool blue eyes from her son over to their newest guests.

Corona caught a waiter passing by and grabbed herself a new drink. It wasn't until she tossed it back and glanced at her parents, that she thought that perhaps she should have offered to get them something to drink, too.

"I want to introduce you to Chloe's parents, Mr. and Mrs. Banks."

"That's Rufus and Adele to you," her father corrected and then cut another nervous glance at Corona. "After all, we're about to be family now. Right?"

Corona glanced around for another waiter, but none were visible at the moment.

"Ahh. Rufus and Adele. I'm pleased to see that you received my invitation."

Corona's head swung back and forth. "What?"

"Yes, we did," her mother answered, smiling. "It was so nice of you to reach out to us."

"Wait a minute," Corona said, wishing that she hadn't been so hasty in chugging down her champagne. "*You* invited them?"

The corners of Wahida's smile nearly touched both ears. "Of course, dear. What kind of engagement party would it be without inviting your parents?"

"Excuse me," said a member of the party staff as he appeared with a broom and dust pan to clean up the glass.

Corona stepped back. Her past and her future were all colliding too fast. She reached out for something to hold on to, but all she could find was Wahida's skeleton-thin bones that were amazingly iron-hard.

"Surprise," Wahida sang, looking like The Joker.

"I don't understand. How?"

Wahida patted her arm. "Oh, it wasn't easy finding your folks, *Corona Mae*."

Corona's knees buckled.

"At first, I kept running into a brick wall until a dear friend of mine suggested that I simply hire a private investigator." Wahida lightly smacked her forehead. "So simple. Anyway, I got Casey Attwater on the phone and twenty-four hours later, I had all your little skeletons dug out of your closet."

All? Corona stared at the woman open-mouthed.

"So am I going to get a hug any time soon or did I waste a couple airline tickets and a trip to that fancy men's store y'all got downtown?" her father asked, opening his arms for a second time.

Corona blinked—not because she didn't want to launch herself into her father's arms, but because she was afraid of what would happen if she did. It'd been so long.

"Honey?" Rowan elbowed her and then gave her a gentle push. It proved to be just the jumpstart she needed to enter her father's arms. But, even so, she was completely unprepared for the dam that had been repressing her emotions for years to completely crumble.

"Corona Mae." Her father sighed next to her ear as his arms tightened around her. "It's been way too long."

Hug him back. You should hug him back. Quivering like the last fall leaf on the first day of winter, Corona drew in a deep breath and then slowly slid her arms around her father, careful not to drop her empty champagne glass.

Rufus Banks's mountainous body trembled as a choked sob escaped him.

Corona's sob wasn't far behind his. Never in her life had she ever come close to seeing her father like this. He had two modes: congenial and angry. One thing he didn't do was cry. He certainly hadn't cried when he'd given her an ultimatum and then disowned her after her great escape from her shotgun wedding.

"I've dreamed of this moment for so long," her mother said, throwing her arms around them in one big bear hug.

Corona's emotional flood was about to test the waterproof claims of her makeup.

"Hey, guys. Don't forget about me."

At the familiar lyrical voice, Corona lifted her head from the crook of her father's arms to see her sister's smiling face.

"Tess." Corona lit up and pulled out of her father's arms so that she could go to her sister next. This unexpected reunion was starting to feel like an episode of *This Is Your Life.* There was just one person missing.

As if the universe had heard her thoughts, Lyfe Alton suddenly appeared at the doorway with a casual smile. She pulled out of her sister's arms, with her eyes wide and her mouth opened in shock.

"Hello, Corona Mae," he said in a warm baritone that nearly melted the muscles off her bones.

Corona's champagne glass crashed to the floor for the second time.

Chapter 10

How Corona remained on her feet was a complete scientific mystery. One would think that other bodily functions would cease to work after going brain-dead, as Corona was sure she had.

"I take it that you're surprised to see me," Lyfe said. His sexy full lips stretched into a breathtaking smile. The baby face was gone and, in its place, was a devastatingly handsome man with a square jaw and glittering cognac-brown eyes.

Corona continued to stand there like a deaf mute while her gaze roamed over Lyfe's rich mahogany skin, his broad shoulders, and his chest that was a landscape of chiseled muscles.

"Hello." Tess waved a hand in front of her face a few times until she broke through her trance.

"Oh. Uh…" She shook her head but the image of Lyfe

and Tess remained in front of her. It wasn't a hallucination.

Tess smiled. "Aren't you going to invite us in?"

Instinctively, Corona shook her head, but said, "Sure. C'mon in."

Lyfe and Tess looked at each other and then back at Corona.

"It's kind of hard to do that with you blocking the door," her sister informed her.

"Oh!" She jumped and then stepped back, crunching down on the broken glass. She picked her foot up too quickly and suddenly felt herself starting to fall backward.

Lyfe's old football instincts kicked into gear, and he rushed into action before her action-star fiancé even had a chance to move.

Strong, sinewy arms wrapped around Corona. There was no doubt in her mind that it was their strength and not the sudden loss of altitude that stole her breath. When he lifted her back up, his masculine scent enveloped her and his intense gaze branded her soul.

Rowan cleared his throat.

One side of Lyfe's full lips cocked into a half smile. "Careful. We don't want you to hurt yourself, now do we?"

She could only mouth the word "no" because her voice failed her. Who cared that there was a house full of people behind her witnessing this…reunion. All she knew was that she could easily spend the rest of her life locked in this man's arms and smothered in his masculine scent. All too soon, he had righted her back onto her feet and unwound his steely arms from her body. But it hadn't stopped her head from spinning.

"It's good seeing you again." He stepped back.

Corona's vertigo intensified.

Rowan wrapped his arm around her waist and sized Lyfe up from head to toe. It was clear in his body language that he sensed a threat.

"I take it that you two know each other," Wahida finally said with a calculating glance. "Quite well, I'm guessing."

Corona thought it was best to ignore that loaded comment. "Uhm, hon—" she cut a look over at Lyfe. "Rowan, this is my sister Contessa."

"But everyone calls me Tess," her sister informed him, stretching out her hand.

"Sister?" Rowan blinked before his smile stretched wider. "Well, give me a hug, sis," he said, flinging his arms open and erasing the short distance between them.

Tess's eyes popped when Rowan lifted her off her feet with a huge bear hug.

While they were doing that, Corona and Lyfe's eyes re-engaged. She tried her best to read him, but she didn't know Lyfe the man like she had known the boy he'd been. Try as she might, she couldn't detect any hint of anger or resentment on his face or even his body language.

Luckily, another waiter strolled by and Corona pounced on one of the passing flutes. When Rowan and Tess broke away, Corona sensed that her fiancé was waiting for her to finish the introductions.

Her gaze shifted to Lyfe and once again her brain frizzed out. "And this is, uhm…er…"

Lyfe's brows crashed together as he realized he would have to introduce himself. "Lyfe Alton. Pleased to meet you." The men smacked palms and shook.

It might have just been Corona, but it appeared to her that Lyfe was pumping and squeezing Rowan's hand with a little more aggression and strength than was necessary.

"Lyfe Alton," Wahida said, rolling the name around her tongue like it was a familiar taste.

For a brief moment, Corona feared the woman was going to put all of Corona's business out in the open. If she had hired a private detective to find her parents, surely she had dug up everything else about her life. Hell, maybe it was her detective that had been snooping around in her closet.

Corona sucked in a deep breath. This just confirmed what she had always suspected: Wahida didn't like her. She didn't know whether it was because of her color, her status, or simply because she wasn't Danica Foxx.

Before the drama Wahida had cooked up could escalate, the crowd behind started tapping their champagne flutes, and the sound rose to a deafening crescendo.

Rowan straightened his shoulders and popped his collar. "That's our signal." Rowan winked at his future in-laws and then grabbed Corona's hand. "Excuse us, won't you?"

Corona didn't know what was happening, and she didn't get a chance to ask before she was whisked away from the small group. As she zipped past Lyfe, once again their gazes connected. A new army of goose bumps marched down her spine, while inside she endured a combination of fluttering butterflies and stomach muscles looping into sailor's knots. And yet, she still couldn't detect anything in his expression.

Why was he there?

Rowan held up his hand to quiet all the clinking

glasses. Then one of the performers handed him a microphone.

"Thanks, everybody. First of all, Chloe and I want to thank each and every one of you for coming out and spending one of your holiday evenings with us on this joyous occasion. For those of you who don't know, this lovely woman standing next to me has agreed to become my wife."

Everyone "aw'ed" and then applauded enthusiastically.

Corona couldn't stop her gaze from scanning out into the crowd. Once she'd zeroed in on Lyfe, she struggled to pull her eyes away. Damn he looked good. He'd smelled good too—and the way his arms felt wrapped around her body was still doing something to her.

From the corner of her eyes, she caught Wahida's head swiveling between her and Lyfe. A couple of times, she even leaned over and whispered something into Danica's ear.

Corona finally found the strength to jerk herself out of her own trance and return her attention to Rowan. But that didn't mean that she could truly concentrate on what he was saying. There was something about his leaving to put in a couple of weeks shooting his next film before the wedding.

Like most men, he was leaving the planning of the wedding to Chloe and his mother. That last part caught Corona's attention and she wondered why in the hell he thought his mother would have any say in *her* wedding. But she covered up her irritation by flashing another smile and then mentally urging Rowan to hurry up and finish. She needed another drink.

But Rowan loved being the center of attention and if

she let him, he would keep them standing there for the rest of the night. "Okay, honey. I think everyone would like to sample some of that wonderful food your mother had catered."

"Ah. That's my cue," Rowan said, winking. "My baby is trying out her new set of balls and chains."

The crowd laughed.

Rowan pulled Corona closer. "I'm a lucky man," he announced and then received another round applause. "Not only am I getting a beautiful wife, but I'm also acquiring a new family. Everyone, I'd like to introduce you all to my new in-laws, the Banks." He gestured to the back of the room. "Rufus, Adele and Tess, raise your hands so everyone can see you."

Oh, dear God, Corona thought.

Everyone turned and her father politely lifted his hand and waved to the crowd. "Pleased to meet y'all," he said in a thick Southern accent.

There were a few giggles that danced through the crowd and Corona grew instantly defensive. Her polite smile twisted into a sharp glower.

However, her parents just smiled, clueless that they were the butt of an unspoken joke.

"And now, I'd like to give *y'all* a preview of coming attractions," Rowan said.

Before Corona had a chance to even guess what the hell he was talking about, she was swept into his arms and dipped so far back that her head nearly touched the floor. When she opened her mouth to protest, it was quickly silenced by Rowan's dramatic kiss. Too bad it wasn't the primary cause of her being lightheaded. That had more to do with him leaving her upside down a few seconds too long. Just as quickly as he dipped her back, he jerked her back up and then released her to wobble on her legs before the crowd.

Lyfe stood stone-faced for about as long as he could stand it before turning toward Tess. "I'm leaving." He pivoted to bolt toward the door.

"No!" Tess latched on to his arm. "You can't leave now."

"Are you kidding me? I think I need my head examined for letting you talk me into coming here. She's getting married—to *that* guy." His face twisted at the thought that she preferred that Tom Cruise wannabe over him. Really? What did that guy have that he didn't?

Another round of amused laughter dusted throughout the crowd before a final applause allowed Rowan to give up the microphone.

"Engaged isn't the same thing as married," Tess reminded him.

He cocked his head at her strange response. "I didn't come here to bust her relationship. I just came to finally get some answers. Closure. That's all." He glanced over his shoulder to take another peek at the happy couple.

Jealousy like he'd never known before twisted in his gut as he watched Rowan ease his arm around Corona's waist in an obvious show of possession. Reflexively Lyfe's hands balled at his sides.

"Just came for some answers, huh?" Tess chuckled as she finally managed to snatch a flute of champagne for herself.

"I think I'm entitled to a few," he said, still tracking the newly engaged couple as they laughed and mingled with their guests. He couldn't help but note just how much more beautiful Corona was in person. The television interview had failed to do her justice.

The girl he'd fallen in love with was gone and, in her place, was this gorgeous creature with incredible Coke bottle curves, long powerful legs and a smile that kept stabbing him in the heart each time she flashed it at everyone but him.

Tess attempted to cut into his thoughts again. "Call me crazy if you want, but, if you ask me, I think you're just trying to punk out."

Lyfe jerked back around and twisted up his face. "Punk out?"

She nodded. "I'm not blind, you know. You haven't been able to keep your eyes off her since you walked in here."

At that moment, Corona snuck a look over at them.

"And apparently she can't keep her eyes off you, either," Tess added.

Lyfe cut another look across the room and sucked in a small breath when his gaze connected with hers. He attributed the extra kick in his pulse to the fact that her eyes had turned a simmering amber color, which meant that she was excited or tuned on. The only problem was that he didn't know whether it was him, or the man standing next to her, that was triggering the reaction.

"Hello, again," Wahida said, cutting back through the crowd. "I hope you guys didn't think that I'd abandoned my special guests."

Lyfe pulled in a deep breath and looked down at the petite older woman. Though he'd been on his guard since he'd walked into this huge SoHo apartment, he added a few more bricks to his protective wall as the woman's calculating gaze unabashedly sized him up.

"Lyfe, isn't it?" she asked.

"Yes, ma'am," he answered, without bothering to smile.

"Interesting name."

Slowly, Lyfe's brows crept upward. Why was this little woman inspecting him like he was standing on an auction block?

"I'm sorry," she said as if reading his thoughts. "I don't mean to stare, but you really are a very handsome man. If I was younger…" She winked.

Is she serious?

Tess slapped a hand over her mouth to prevent herself from laughing and spewing out her champagne. She quickly covered it up by turning around and joining a small group behind her that included her parents.

"Thank you," Lyfe said, downgrading his own laughter to just a small smile.

"I'm sorry, but I think that I missed hearing about your association with Chloe."

He cringed. "Frankly, I don't know a Chloe."

Wahida perked up. "Oh, really?"

"I knew her as Corona Mae," he clarified. "I grew up with the Bankses in Thomason."

"I see," she said. "So you two are just—"

"Friends," Corona cut in, and then cast a look at Lyfe that asked him to back her up on this.

He refused to grant or deny her silent request. He just stood there on mute, willing to let her hang herself with this one.

Corona got the picture. "Uh, Wahida, will you excuse me and Lyfe for a moment?" She gently slid her arm underneath Lyfe's and attempted to pull him away.

He remained rooted where he stood and casually looked down at how she was tugging him. It was a gentle enough pull, but her touch felt like a firebrand burning through his clothes. His heart pounded so loud it drowned out the Christmas music.

"It will just take a second," she pressed with a nervous smile.

Wahida lifted a brow at the tension between them.

"It's okay," Tess said, as she returned to the group. "I'll wait right here for you."

Corona's parents joined them.

"Actually," her father said, clearing his throat, "I was hoping to get a few minutes alone with you, Corona Mae."

Corona's hand tightened on Lyfe's bicep.

There was also a look that flickered across her face that cracked the wall around Lyfe's heart. *Damn. Am I even prepared to hear the answers to my questions?*

"Here. You're going to need this," Tess said, handing him a drink.

He took the flute. "Thanks."

Rowan eased into the circle. "Honey, you're starting to be a little difficult to keep up with this evening."

Corona's hand slipped from underneath Lyfe's arm, and he immediately missed it.

"Sorry about that, sweetheart. I was just…trying to catch up with my family and…"

"So you're *friends?*" Wahida said, with her eyes narrowing and swinging suspiciously between Corona and Lyfe.

As if sensing her sister needed help, Tess cleared her throat and stepped closer. "Actually, he's more than just her friend."

Surprised, Lyfe and Corona's brows jumped.

"Contessa, sweetheart." her father cut in, with a warning look.

"Oh?" Wahida said, edging closer.

Ignoring everyone, Tess threw up her chin and eased her arm underneath Lyfe's other arm. She was ready to tell the biggest lie of her life. "Yes. He's going to be her brother-in-law. We're engaged."

Corona's third champagne glass crashed against the floor.

Chapter 11

"You're...what?" Corona asked. Surely something was wrong with her ears. There was no way her sister had just said what she'd thought she said. She just couldn't have.

However, Tess's smile stretched wider as she leaned against Lyfe's chest. "Surprise!"

Corona's gaze flew to Lyfe's face but, once again, she couldn't read anything in his stony expression. "Excuse me. I...need to go...check on something." With that she turned and raced through the crowd.

She was vaguely aware of a few people calling her name, but all she could think about was getting some fresh air. With no other recourse, she plowed out onto the snow-covered terrace and chugged in deep breaths. She didn't even feel the cold. *Engaged?*

She clutched a hand over her chest and hoped that it was enough to keep her heart from trying to pound its way out. After a full minute, she still wasn't sure whether the deep breaths were quite doing the job. "How could Tess do something like this to me?"

"Something like what?"

At the sound of Lyfe's deep baritone, Corona spun around. "I, uh…" What could she say? *How could Tess steal my man?* He was no longer hers—hadn't been for a long time. As her gaze took another lap over his impressive frame, regret rose like a wave and crashed like a tsunami against her heart.

Lyfe closed the terrace door.

She panicked. "What are you doing?"

"I'm sure that it's considered rude to try and freeze your guests," he answered smoothly.

She guessed that made sense.

Lyfe slid his hands into his pockets and strolled toward her.

Corona backed up and ignored the fact that snow was sliding into her pumps.

He cocked his head. "I'm not making you nervous, am I?"

"Of course not," she lied.

A corner of his lips curled. "Good. The last thing I want to do is make you feel uncomfortable in your own home."

By the time he stopped in front of her, Corona was holding on to a frozen rail with her head tilted all the way back so that she could maintain eye contact. *Damn. He looks good.* It was hard to get any other thought squeezed into her brain. He completely blew away every actor and model she'd ever met or seen in the industry. There was so much power in his presence that it felt like he was stealing all the oxygen—even though they were outside!

"What are you doing here?" she finally squeaked out of her tight windpipes.

"I was invited," he said simply.

"You know what I mean," she said with a little more courage. "It's been…so long."

"It has," Lyfe said, but he didn't seem to be in any hurry to answer the question. In fact, he looked as if he was content to just drink her in.

And she was content to do the same.

"You're freezing," he noted and then quickly slid off his jacket.

"That's not necessary." Corona hunched up her shoulders, but Lyfe ignored her and swung his jacket around her like a cape. In the next second she was enveloped in both his warmth and his seductive scent. *What the hell is he trying to do to me?*

"There. That's not so bad, is it?" he asked, sliding his hands back into his pockets.

"What about you?"

Lyfe lifted a brow. "You're concerned about my well-being?" He chuckled. "Well, I guess there's a first time for everything."

The gibe was a direct punch to the gut.

"So I take it that you still hate me?"

The question hung between them for what felt like an eternity before he finally said, "No."

"Very convincing," she said, swallowing and glancing off. Normally the city view took her breath away, but tonight the holiday spray of lights just saddened her.

"Would you prefer that I hated you?"

Tears stung the backs of her eyes. *I'd prefer that you hadn't come here.*

"Or maybe you preferred that I hadn't come?"

Corona's head whipped back around. "Are you really engaged to my sister?"

"Would it matter?"

"Of course it matters," she snapped, oblivious that she was teetering on the edge of irrationality.

He erased the last step between them until their chests bumped together. Suddenly, it was like being plugged into an electric socket. The jolt they experienced had their bodies tingling from the electricity between them.

Dizzy, Corona took another step back and unplugged from their powerful connection.

While she tried to get her bearings, Lyfe confessed, "I tried to hate you."

She met his gaze.

He nodded. "For a long time, in fact. I never really pulled it off. I wish that I could understand why. I mean, I foolishly thought that, at the bare minimum, we were friends. But that couldn't have been true. A friend would have at least left a note."

It felt like her tears turned into battery acid. "I did what I thought was best. I did it for you—us."

He shook his head. "No. You did it for you. You wanted out of that town and you wanted to get as far away from me as you possibly could. I get it. And look…" He stepped back as well. "You've done real good for yourself. You're running a big-time talent agency and now you're about to marry the number one box office star. Life is good."

"No. You got it all wrong."

"What? You're not a big success? You haven't achieved everything that you've ever dreamed of?" There was a hardness that was slowly creeping into his eyes.

"Of course not." *Because we're not together.* "It's… complicated."

While that statement hung between them, the temperature seemed to drop another ten degrees.

"Complicated," he finally repeated and then glanced off toward the scenic view. "I traveled all the way up here to New York just for you to tell me that it's…complicated?"

Corona opened her mouth to respond, but all that she could manage to get past her lips were thin puffs of cold air.

"Well, that's disappointing." He drew in a deep breath and then reached over and removed his jacket from around her shoulders. "Good luck to you." With that, he turned and strolled back toward the terrace door.

Icy tears trickled down Corona's face as she watched Lyfe walk away. "What would you have me say?" she asked.

He stopped with his hand on the door. "That's just it. I don't know." Lyfe glanced over his shoulder. "But it sure wasn't some bullshit like 'it's complicated.'" He jerked open the door and strolled back inside.

Corona blinked and then tried to hold back her tears. It turned out to be a pretty hard task now that Lyfe's mere presence was like an emotional nuclear bomb exploding in her heart. She had long thought that he was out her life—that they would never see each other again—that their paths would never cross.

And now he was here.

At long last, the night's cold penetrated her bones, forcing her to go back into the apartment. This time, when she moved through the crowd, she had trouble painting on a smile. However, she had no trouble spotting Lyfe as he made it back to the small circle of Rowan and her family. She watched with her heart in her throat as he leaned down and whispered something into Tess's ear.

Immediately, the two sisters' gazes met from across the room. Lyfe started for the door, but Tess grabbed his arm and then rolled up on her toes to whisper something into his ear.

Jealousy rose like a dragon inside Corona's heart. She had the urge to march back over to the group herself and snatching every strand of hair out of Tess's head. Wahida may have laid this trap, but, for the first time, she noticed the calculating look on her sister's face.

Rowan said something to Lyfe, but Lyfe shook his head. Whatever excuse he was giving, her fiancé wasn't trying to hear it. The men went back and forth, and then Tess and her parents got in on it until Lyfe's shoulders slumped and he nodded.

Rowan lit up and then gave Lyfe a one arm hug before spinning around and spotting her across the room. "Honey, come here." He waved her over.

Corona groaned and, for a brief second, she thought about pretending not to have seen him. But with the whole family looking and staring her dead in the face, she tried to inject steel into her spine and give herself a pep talk as she made her way back through the crowd. As she got closer, she noticed that Lyfe averted his eyes and gritted his teeth.

"We have a great idea to swing by you, honey,"

Rowan said, slipping an arm around her waist and planting a kiss against the side of her head.

Lyfe finally glanced over.

"Is that right?" she said, leaning into Rowan for support.

Rowan nodded and continued, "What do you think about us being in each other's weddings?" he asked.

She blinked up at him.

"Tess was going to be your maid of honor, right? I figured Lyfe here can be my best man and then when they get married in January—"

"January?" Corona whipped her head toward her sister.

Tess shrugged. "What better way to start off a new year than walking down the aisle?"

Corona clenched her jaw while another image of her yanking her sister bald-headed flashed across her head.

"Perfect," Rowan said. "They will be in our wedding, and then we'll be in theirs. What do you think?"

Corona's skittish gaze made its way back to Lyfe before she pushed up another painful smile. "I guess you're right. It's perfect."

Chapter 12

"So you think that this Lyfe guy is your father?" Amanda Hogan asked, twisting up her face as she leaned over Melody's shoulder.

"He just has to be," Melody said, flopping back onto one of Amanda's fluffy pillows. She clutched two of her mother's diaries to her chest and smiled dreamily up at the ceiling. "I never knew that my mother had ever been in love like this before. It's soooo...unlike her."

"For real," Carrie Jones said dismissively. "I've always thought that it was more appropriate for her to marry her job."

Melody sat up and felt the need to come to her mother's defense. "All right. That's not fair. She's not completely a workaholic. She never missed a recital or school play. And somehow she still manages to check my homework and watch my every move like a hawk."

Amanda and Carrie laughed. "Still sore that you got

caught sneaking out of the house to see Robbie back in August?"

"I am," Melody grudgingly admitted. "I'm only just now getting off restriction." Another smile curled her lips. "But at least I got to see Robbie before he left to be an exchange student in Paris. So it was kind of worth it. Plus, while I was bored in the house, I was able to find her secret stash." She sat up and glanced down at the diaries. "I thought my mother didn't understand what I was feeling but after reading these diaries…she understands perfectly. She loved this Lyfe more than…life itself," she cracked up at the small joke. "They were so in love."

"Sounds to me like you're practically willing this guy to be your father," Carrie said. She grabbed one of the other books and started flipping through the pages.

Now feeling possessive, Melody grabbed the book from her best friend. "No, I'm not. I'm just facing the facts. Their whole love affair fits the timeline to my birthday."

Carrie continued to look unconvinced. "They only did it that one time. Who's to say that she didn't come to New York and shack up with a new boyfriend?"

Melody laughed at the ludicrous thought. "Are you kidding me? My mother is not the type. Heck. Rowan James is the first real boyfriend that I've even known her to have." She opened her mother's journals again. "No. There's no mention of another guy in here the year I was born. This Lyfe Alton has to be him."

"What has your mother ever told you about your father?"

Melody's shoulders drooped. "Only that things hadn't worked out between them and that one day when I'm older she'll tell me all about him." She started hugging the books again. "Now she doesn't have to."

Amanda sighed. "Well, if you ask me, none of what you've read to us sounds like your mother. She's so no-nonsense, and she's always running five minutes late for everything with a phone attached to her ear. In those diaries, she sort of sounds like…us."

Melody nodded. Inwardly she acknowledged that since she had started reading these diaries, she'd felt closer to her mom. She felt like she understood her on a deeper level. Except for why she was about to marry a man she didn't love. Rowan James was just some actor on the rebound. Even she could see that.

"So what are you going to do now?" Carrie asked.

"What else? I'm going to find him."

"Engaged?" Rufus barked. His face was puffing up and turning purple as he climbed into the back of their limousine. His sharp accusing gaze sliced over to Lyfe. "What? You like playing eeny-meeny-miny-moe between my daughters?"

Lyfe's collar tightened as his own temper flared.

"Wait," Tess said, jumping in before a full-fledged war broke out. "Calm down, Daddy," she said. "We're not engaged. I lied."

Adele gasped and then covered her mouth with her hands.

Her father raged on, "I want to make it clear that I've *never* liked…" Tess's words finally penetrated his angry fog. "You what?" he asked, jerking his head in Tess's direction.

"I lied," Tess repeated as if it was no big deal. "I

wanted to see whether I was right about something…
and I think I am."

Adele shook her head. "But to say that Melody's f—"

"Mom, it's just an experiment." Tess's eyes narrowed
to remind her mother that Corona's secrets weren't theirs
to share.

Adele caught the hint and then quickly pressed her
lips together.

Rufus remained indignant. "I don't like it! I don't
like it. After twenty-something years of you sitting in
the front pew, listening to my sermons, you think it's
okay to toss around lies like this?"

"Oh, Daddy. Calm down," Tess said. "I'll tell her the
truth. Right now, I want to see what she does next."

Lyfe finally cleared his throat. "Well, you'll have
to finish your experiment without me. I'm on the next
plane out of here." He glanced out of the back window,
wishing their driver would hurry and get them back to
their hotel. He had certainly had more drama than he
could possibly stand for one night.

"You can't leave now," Tess said, grabbing his arm.
"You saw how she reacted when she saw you. She's not
over you."

He shook his head. "I didn't come here to win her
back, Tess. You know that. I came for answers…and I
got them."

"You did?" the Banks clan asked in unison.

"Yeah. She said it was…complicated." His top lip
curled with a wrinkle of disgust. "Good to know, don't
you think?"

The limo fell silent. Lyfe appreciated the silence as he
took in the city's ornate holiday theme. When he was a
kid, he used to love the Christmas holidays. There were

so many memories of him and Corona being in Christmas plays, going door-to-door caroling and even building snowmen and having snowball fights. Their love of the holidays had been one of the many reasons they had chosen this time of the year to finally become lovers. It was supposed to have been just one more happy memory to associate with the holidays.

Now the holidays brought him nothing but pain.

At long last the limousine rolled to a stop in front of the Four Seasons hotel, and Lyfe popped out of the back seat the moment the valet opened the door. But, though he would love to do nothing more than to give the Banks his back while he stormed through the hotel's front door, he turned and offered a hand to Tess to help her out of the car. "Regardless of how this night ended, I do want to thank you for talking me into coming. I think that I'm finally able to close this last chapter with Corona Mae."

"But—"

"Not only that, but I'm going to take a page out of her book and move on." He leaned forward and brushed a kiss against her forehead. "Take care of yourself, kid."

Rufus and Adele climbed out of the back and Lyfe tipped his head. "Goodbye, Mr. and Mrs. Banks." He turned and finally strolled into the hotel.

"But, Lyfe, wait," Tess shouted.

He ignored her call, determined to finally leave the Bankses firmly in his past.

Chapter 13

It had been years since Corona had woken up hungover. From the moment she attempted to open her eyes, there was some invisible devil at the back of her skull with a jackhammer, pounding away. Her battle to open her eyes only lasted a quarter of a second before she gave up the fight and told herself to lie as still as humanly possible. However, that tiny devil and his jackhammer were merciless and continued to drill. With one burst of energy, Corona flung out a hand, hoping to hit Rowan. But the other side of the bed was empty. So much for her plan of getting her fiancé to pity her enough to bring her some Excedrin and water. But there was some relief in not having him around to pester her about last night.

Last night.

Her family and Lyfe Alton showing up at her engagement party unannounced just had to have been a dream...or a nightmare. She couldn't decide on which one just yet.

Riiiiiiinnnnnng!

Forget the jackhammer. The phone was a nuclear bomb that launched her straight up out of the bed. Even with her eyes wide open, it still took her a few seconds of looking around to recognize her own bedroom. Why had she thought that she had fallen asleep at Rowan's place?

Riiiiiiinnnnng!

Corona's temples detonated, causing her to slap her hands to the sides of her head to make sure that the damn thing was still attached. She was actually surprised that it was. The phone was starting to gear up for the third ring when she finally reached over and snatched up the cordless phone.

"Yeah. What is it?" It wasn't the most cordial way to answer the phone, but she certainly wanted to convey to the caller that they should keep it brief.

"Momma?"

The migraine, nausea and her foul mood were quickly tossed out of the window. "Melody, baby? What is it?" She glanced around for the digital clock. "What time is it?" *Heck. What day was it?*

"It's just noon," Melody informed her. "How was the engagement party?"

Corona moaned before she had a chance to stop herself.

"That doesn't sound too good," Melody perked up.

"It...was...interesting." She slid her hands into her tussled hair while she tried to process everything that had happened. But when her brain made it clear that it wasn't even going to attempt to figure out the whole

Lyfe and Tess engagement, she changed the subject. "What time is Amanda's mother bringing you home? I'm thinking we should have lunch so we can talk." *Especially before you see your grandparents...and possibly your father.*

"Well, that's what I was calling you about. Is it okay that I stay an extra night here? We were thinking about spending the day Christmas shopping, and I can't shop for your gift with you around."

"An extra night?" She hesitated for a second. But maybe she needed this time to confront Tess and her parents alone, so that she could at least get her story straight for her daughter.

"Please, Momma. Carrie is here, too, and we all just want to hang out for the day."

"All right. Just one more night. Let me speak to Amanda's mother to make sure that it's all right with her."

"Yea! Thanks, Mom. You're the greatest."

Corona rolled her eyes with a smile. A few months ago her daughter had been declaring her the worst mother in the world when she'd been grounded after sneaking out of the house to see some boy. It had been the worst four hours of Corona's life as she'd sat thinking of all the missing-child horror stories that usually played out on the evening news. That prank had landed Miss Melody on three months of restriction.

A minute later, Melody's cell phone was passed over to Mrs. Hogan who verified and okayed the extra day at her home. Once the phone was handed back to her daughter, Corona extracted a promise from Melody to be on her best behavior then ended the call.

She now had twenty-four hours to get to the bottom

of what was going on, and she wasn't about to waste a single moment of it. Peeling herself out of her bedding, Corona was surprised to see that she was still wearing last night's dress, complete with her Prada shoes. When she stood, she quickly realized that heels were not the best option when hungover. Neither was hopping around, trying to get them off.

In the bedroom's adjoining bathroom, she took one glance at her reflection, then quickly turned away before she turned herself into stone. It wasn't until she was standing beneath the shower's streaming hot water that she got any relief. Just how much champagne had she drank?

Two hours later, she looked decent enough to rejoin the human race, plus she'd downed enough coffee to keep an elephant awake for at least half a year. She did at least remember her mother mentioning that they were all staying at the Four Seasons. It wasn't until now that she wondered how they could afford such a luxury.

Wahida. Corona groaned. It stood to reason that if she had invited them all up to New York that she would also provide their accommodations.

"Why does that woman hate me?" she asked, racing out her front door. When she hopped into the back of the Maybach and dug out her cell phone, she saw that she had over twenty-three missed calls—most of them from her assistant Margo. She started to hit her callback option, but then pulled herself back. If she called the office, then chances were that she was going to spend the day dealing with actors and putting out small fires with studios.

No. Today she was going to play hooky.

"Where to, ma'am?" the driver asked.

"The Four Seasons," she answered, plopping her phone back into her purse. "Please make it quick."

Lyfe had spent the rest of his night making himself some long overdue promises. Number one being that he was now going to commit to finding a woman to settle down with. He was a successful architect, and it was time for him to become a family man. By the time he'd finally managed to fall asleep, he was content with his new life decision. When he woke up, he felt rejuvenated. A quick call to the airport informed him that there were no available flights out that morning, but he was more than welcome to wait to fly standby. His other option was to take a late afternoon flight. That was okay by him, as long he was back in his own bed by that night.

With his suitcase open on the bed, he started the work of repacking his belongings. A couple of seconds later, there was knock on his door. Since housekeeping had already been by, he concluded that it was Tess and waffled on whether he should open it.

Knock! Knock!

"C'mon, bro. I know that you're in there."

Lyfe blinked at the sound of Hennessey's voice on the other side.

"What on earth?" He dropped his small stack of shirts and strolled over to the door. When he opened it up, he was still in shock. "What on earth are you doing here?"

"Oh, I was just…flying around the neighborhood," Hennessey said, strolling into the room. "Figured that I'd just drop by."

"Is that right?" Lyfe released the door and let it slam shut behind his brother. "Since I know that you don't own a plane or particularly care for New Yorkers, you want to try that again?"

Hennessey ignored the question. "Packing?"

"Very good observation. Now do you want to answer the question?"

"I thought I did," he said, pulling out the stack of shirts that Lyfe had just put in the suitcase.

"What are you doing?"

"Helping you unpack."

Lyfe strolled over to the bed and took the shirts out of his brother's arms. "I just called the airport. I have a six o'clock flight."

Hennessey took back the shirts. "Cancel it."

"Give me a break. What? Did Tess put you up to this?"

"Can't a concerned brother just show up and help you do the right thing?"

Lyfe crossed his arms and leveled him with a dubious look.

"I'm hurt. Deeply," Hennessey said, pressing his hand against his chest.

"I'm sure you'll get over it."

"And I'm sure that if you jump on that six o'clock flight that you'll regret it for the rest of your life."

"I'm already regretting that I even came here," Lyfe said.

Hennessey swept his arm around his brother's shoulder. "Aww. C'mon. You don't mean that."

Lyfe pinched the bridge of his nose and huffed out a long breath. It looked like his starting a new chapter in his life was going to have to wait.

"Aww. C'mon. Don't look like that. At least I'm here

to keep you company," Hennessey boasted, whacking him on the back. "Have you had lunch yet?"

"I was going to pick something up at the airport."

"Well, since that's out the question, what do you say that we go and grab something to eat?"

What choice did he have? His brother certainly didn't know how to take no for an answer.

"Hey, we don't even have to leave the hotel. There's a nice restaurant downstairs."

"Fine. Fine." Lyfe shrugged off his brother's arm. "I still say that Tess put you up to this."

Hennessey slapped a hand over his heart. "You wound me. Truly."

Lyfe was accustomed to his brother faking innocence so he just ignored him and soldiered on out the door.

Behind him, Hennessey scooped out his cell phone and speed dialed Tess. "The cat is in the cradle," he whispered into the receiver then quickly hung up.

Chapter 14

Tess smiled as she hummed the theme song of *Mission: Impossible.* She absolutely loved a challenge—almost as much as she loved messing around in other folks' business. And as far as she was concerned, mucking around in her sister's business was a long overdue project. The way she saw it, Corona Mae may have become a success in the business world, but when it came to her personal life she was flying high with blinders on. After last night, it was clear to her that Lyfe also had on his own blinders. However, if he thought his little announcement last night was going to throw a monkey wrench in her plans, then he clearly didn't know who he was dealing with.

She was a semiprofessional matchmaker. Of course there were a few potholes she'd need to avoid, and there was the potential for a blow up when Lyfe found out that he had a daughter. But if he still felt the way she believed he did about her sister, the end result would be those two finally tying the knot. It certainly wasn't easy getting her parents to go along, but she knew that they secretly wanted the same thing.

Just when she was about to make her umpteenth call to her sister's cell, her niece's number and smiling face popped up on her Android phone. Surprised, she answered the call. "Now what's my favorite niece in the whole wide world doing? Did your mother tell you that me and your grandparents are in town?"

"You're in town?" Melody asked excitedly. "Where are you at? Are you at my house?"

"Oh? You mean she didn't tell you?"

"No. I'm not home. I'm at a friend's house. Did you just get here?"

"No. Uhm, we arrived last night. We went to your mother's engagement party."

"Oh." Melody's excitement took a major nosedive. "I guess that means that you finally met *him*."

Tess's brows leapt up. "You mean Rowan James? What? You don't like your future stepfather?"

"I think he likes himself enough for the both of us," Melody droned.

Tess laughed. "Well, I really didn't get too much of a chance to get to know him. The place was pretty crowded."

"Don't waste your time. I don't really think he'll be around that long. Rebound relationships never last."

"Ouch. That's a pretty harsh assessment for someone your age," she said, even though she agreed with her niece.

"I may be young, but the same thing goes on in school. If you meet a guy right after he's gone through a crushing breakup, chances are you're the rebound girl. Plus, I'm not convinced Momma is really in love with him anyway."

"Oh?" Tess's ear perked up at this insider information. "Why do you say that?"

"Well," Melody hedged, "I said something to her a few months back that…maybe I shouldn't have."

This was getting juicier. "What did you say?"

Her niece hesitated.

"Melody," Tess prodded. "What did you say?"

"Well, first of all, I was upset. See, I really like this boy Robbie."

She remembered the name. "You mean the little boy you snuck out of the house to see in the middle of the night?"

"He was leaving for Paris for a whole year! I just wanted to say goodbye to him."

"Uh-huh."

"Well, anyway. Momma freaked out and grounded me for like forever and I…"

"And you what?"

"Well, I shouted at her how much I hated her and that she was mean and was probably going to die alone."

Tess gasped.

"I didn't mean it. I was just angry."

"So you tried to hurt her? Melody, that was a terrible thing to say to your mother."

"I know," she groaned.

"You have no idea what your mother has been through trying to raise you alone up here in New York."

"Actually," Melody said meekly, "I kind of do. I sort of found her old diaries."

Tess nearly fell off the edge of the bed. "What?"

"See. That's sort of what I was calling you about."
Uh-oh. "Me?"

"Yeah. I was hoping you could tell me about Lyfe Alton and whether you know where he is?"

The ride to the Four Seasons took three times longer than usual. Not because of the snow, because New Yorkers were certainly used to snow in the winter time, but because of the ice. Cars crept along or, in some cases, slid along at a snail's pace. That didn't stop some of them from playing ice bumper cars. Luckily her driver got her to the hotel safely. When she was helped out of the car, a good arctic blast turned her into a popsicle.

Once inside the hotel, she received an equivalent blast of heat that quickly thawed her out.

"Welcome to the Four Seasons. How may I help you?" a woman behind the lobby counter asked.

"Yes. I'm looking for Contessa Banks's room, please."

The front desk clerk picked up the phone. "Your name?"

"Chloe…uhm, better make that Corona Banks."

The woman gave her a look like "don't you know your own name?" But she quickly called up to her sister's room. "Yes. We have a Corona Banks down in the lobby to see you. Yes, ma'am." She hung up and then wrote down the room number. "You can go right up."

"Thank you." Corona flashed a smile and then jogged over to the elevator. Less than a minute later, she stepped out onto the tenth floor and went in search of her sister's room. As she continued to follow the numbers, a door opened.

"Corona Mae?"

Corona turned at the sound of her mother's voice. "Momma?"

Adele rolled out a room service cart and adjusted a bright red silk robe around her waist. And was she still wearing makeup?

Corona blinked several more times because she couldn't recall a single time in her childhood when her mother had worn anything like a silk robe.

"Sweetheart, I'm so glad to see you." She glanced down the hall. "Is Melody with you?"

Corona shook her head while still trying to comprehend her mother's attire.

"Well, no matter. I guess we can see her a little later. Get on in here." She waved her daughter in. "I tried to call you several times this morning."

Corona stepped forward like she was in a trance.

Her mother remained all smiles as she swung her arms around Corona's shoulders and pulled her the rest of the way into their lavish room. No sooner had the door slammed shut than her father came jogging out of the bathroom in a pair of tight red briefs. "Ta-dah!" he said.

Both his and Corona's eyes widened to the size of silver dollars.

"Oh, my God!" He made a quick U-turn and scrambled back into the bathroom. "Adele! Why didn't you tell me Corona Mae was here?"

Adele winced. "Sorry, baby. She just got here," her mother called out.

"I think I need to bleach out my eyes," Corona said, blinking and trying to get the image out of her head.

Her mother took her hand and patted it. "Honey, I'm

so sorry that you had to see your father like that. We've been trying some new things and—"

"Mom, please." Corona kept blinking. "I *really* don't want to know."

"Yes, I guess you don't." She coughed and cleared her throat. "Well, I'm glad you're here. You were so busy with your guests last night that we really didn't get a chance to talk."

"I know, but you guys also unloaded quite a lot on me last night."

"Oh, that." Her mother's mouth twisted downward.

"Yeah. That." Corona folded her arms. "Is Lyfe and Tess's engagement for real?"

"Honey, I think that you should talk to your sister about that."

"I intend to." Corona paced. "The very idea of Tess and Lyfe getting married is…ridiculous. The last thing I heard was that they just bumped into each other like a week ago."

"Well, I don't know if ridiculous is the right word," her mother hedged. "But it would make things rather awkward at family get-togethers. Of course, we have so few of those. With you in New York and Aunt Charlene passed on."

"Awkward? Just awkward?" Corona repeated incredulously. "If they have children, they will be Melody's cousins as well as her siblings."

"That may be, but it's not like Melody knows that Lyfe is her father."

"And how long do you think I'll be able to keep that a secret? The minute he lays eyes on her he's going to know the truth. Melody looks just like him."

Her mother opened her mouth, but she clearly didn't have an answer to that.

"I can't believe you guys brought him here."

"Actually, honey, your father and I didn't have anything to do with it. Your sister acted alone on that one."

"Now *that* I believe."

"Sweetheart, calm down. It's going to be all right. By now, Lyfe is probably back in Atlanta."

Surprise and disappointment dueled inside Corona for a full ten seconds. "Oh."

"See?" Her mother's arms wrapped around her. "Feel better? Now you don't have to worry about father and daughter bumping into each other. Though you know how I feel about that."

She nodded, but then thought, "So does that mean that they're *not* engaged?"

Adele hedged. "You need to talk to your sister."

"That's exactly what I intend to do," she said, turning out of her mother's arms and marching back to the door. "I'll call you a little later."

"But…but…"

"I promise," Corona added and then slipped out of the door.

A second later, she heard her mother shout, "It's alright, Rufus. You can come out now."

Despite her annoyance at her sister, Corona chuckled over seeing her father in his tight red briefs. She knocked on her sister's door and debated whether she should push up a smile or pimp slap her sister into the middle of next week when she answered the door.

She was leaning toward a pimp slap.

Chapter 15

"So let me get this straight," Lyfe said, lowering his napkin into his lap. "You *want* me to talk to Corona Mae again?"

Hennessey shrugged his huge shoulders. "Why not? You flew all the way here. Might as well try and get a real answer."

Lyfe had a hard time swallowing that. "Uh-huh. I see."

"You see what?" Hennessey asked, smirking.

"I see that I'm right. Tess called you and put you up this. What? Did she agree to go out with you or something? You picked a woman over your own flesh and blood?"

"What? I'm just pointing out the obvious. She's in New York. You're in New York."

"And I saw her last night," Lyfe reminded him while trying to get the image of Corona in that stunning dress out of his mind. *Today is a new day. I'm moving on with my life.*

"Look…" Hennessey leaned over their lunch table. "What did you expect her to say in the middle of her engagement party to another man? Of course she gave you some tired line about it all being complicated. The *real* question is whether you detected if she still has feelings for you."

"I'm not here to bust up—"

"Yes you are," Hennessey cut him off. "You lie to yourself on your own time, but when you're talking to me, I'd appreciate it if you were just straight up."

They glared over the table.

Hennessey leaned in even closer. "Look. In honor of keeping it real, I'm going to remind you of something. All in love is fair, man. Things didn't workout between y'all when you were kids for whatever reason, but what did *you* feel when you saw her again?"

"That is beside the point," Lyfe said, shaking his head.

"No. It *is* the point. It takes two to make a relationship, man. Just because I'm not in the market for a ball and chain, doesn't mean that I don't know what I'm talking about. If a man is about to steal someone that you feel rightfully belongs with you, then you need to step up." Hennessey threw some extra bass into his voice.

It was enough to get Lyfe to reconsider everything. Had he been lying to himself? Did he come here to stop a wedding or was he just hoping to stop a wedding?

Hennessey sensed victory. "Look. The way I see it, your girl got scared and ran, but you didn't exactly chase after her. You went home, constructed a big invisible wall around your heart and vowed to never get hurt again. A textbook male reaction. I get it. The whole Brotherhood Nation gets it. But if you can sit there in that chair and tell me with a straight face that *you* didn't feel anything when you saw your old girl, and you honestly don't think that *she* felt anything, then I say you're right. Get your big butt on the next plane out of this icebox city and move on to the next one."

He paused and looked Lyfe directly in the eyes.

"But if you did feel something and you believe she did too, then, as a man, you need to do everything in your power to get back what rightfully belongs to you. You feel me?"

Lyfe let his brother's words sink in and, before he knew it, he was bobbing his head in agreement. "Yeah. I know exactly what you mean."

"Lyfe...who?" Tess stalled her niece over the line. While she had been busy trying to work it out so that father and daughter would soon be introduced, this new scenario could end with her sister literally putting her head on a spike.

"Lyfe Alton. And please don't tell me you never heard of him before. I know that you have."

"Uhm...Melody, sweetheart. I think that is a question that you need to ask your mother."

Silence.

"Melody?"

"He's my father, isn't he?"

Knock! Knock! Knock!

Oh, thank God. "Oh, honey. There's someone at the door. Let me call you back."

"Aunt Tess—"

"I'll call you back. I promise." She disconnected the

call and rushed toward the door. But when she opened it, she quickly wished that she hadn't.

"I'm going to kill you," her sister seethed, hitting the door so that it went flying out of Tess's hands. "How *dare* you pull some stupid prank like this? Do you know what you could've done? What if Melody had been at that party last night? Do you know what kind of mess you could've caused?" As Corona bulldozed her way in, Tess propelled backward across her hotel room.

Tess's hands quickly came up in surrender. "All right. Don't hurt me. I don't have any health insurance."

"When I'm finished with you, you won't need health care, you'll need a tombstone!"

"All right. All right. You're angry. I get it." She'd now backed all the way to the wall. "Maybe…just maybe I didn't think this whole thing through all the way," she reasoned nervously.

"You think? We're not kids anymore, Tess. These types of pranks have serious consequences." Her hands balled at her sides.

Recognizing the signs, Tess covered her head and curled over at her side to prepare for a few blows. Instead, her sister released a long hiss and then stormed away from her.

"You're not worth my ass catching a case."

Tess exhaled loudly as she unfolded herself back up. "Well, thank God for small favors."

"I'm still pissed," Corona warned.

"I know. I know. But if you just let me explain—"

"Look, the only reason I'm not beating you into the carpet is because Lyfe left New York."

"Ehhh…" Tess winced.

Corona Mae's gaze sliced back over to her. "Ehhh, what?"

Knock. Knock. Knock.

"Weeeeeellll." Tess headed over to the door. "There may have been a *slight* change in plan." She opened the door and was swept up into Lyfe's arms.

"Good afternoon, my lovely fiancée." He had swung her around half of the room before he noticed she had company. "Corona."

Chapter 16

Instant tears sprang into Corona's eyes. Her fists unraveled as she bolted toward the door. "I gotta go," she said and nearly plowed headlong into Hennessey's chest. He quickly got out of the way.

"Wait, Corona Mae." Lyfe released Tess. She was about to land on the floor when Hennessey turned and sprinted to catch her. "Corona, let me explain," Lyfe continued, giving chase in the hallway.

Corona ignored him as she raced back to the elevator bay and hit the down button. But when it was clear that Lyfe would catch up to her before the elevator could arrive, she bolted toward the staircase. Lyfe just chased after her.

"Corona, will you please hold up? I just want to talk to you for a few minutes."

"Well, I don't want to talk to you, so you can just go back up to your...fiancée! I hope you two have a wonderful life together." Why in the hell was she wearing heels? It was just a matter of time before...

Her heel clipped the edge of a step and the next thing she knew, she was flying and screaming. Her purse hit the ground and exploded across the stairwell landing. She was about to crash onto the concrete floor, when Lyfe's steel grip suddenly grabbed her. Once she realized she was safe, she finally decided that it would be a good idea for her to give her lungs a rest.

Turning her upright and setting her back on her feet against a concrete wall Lyfe asked, "Are you all right?"

Panting, Corona bobbed her head but refused to meet his steady gaze. But she was very conscious of his warm, minty breath drifting across the shell of her ear.

"You know, that's the second time I've had to catch you in less than twenty-four hours. I don't remember you being so clumsy."

"Clumsy?" Her eyes shot up toward his.

"Ah. Now you can look me in the eye." He pushed up a smile.

The sight of his pearly whites had a devastating effect on her knees, and, for a couple of seconds, she feared that she was doomed to take another tumble. He was standing too close. She couldn't breathe. Instinctively, she placed her hand against his chest in an attempt to push him back, but she may as well have been trying to shove an Army tank up a San Francisco hill.

Lyfe glanced down at her hand, particularly the diamond glittering on it. But then he reached down and moved her hand from the center of his stomach up to his heart, so that she could feel her effect on him.

Corona gasped at the hammering against her palm

and tried to pull her hand back. Lyfe was having none of that and kept it in place. Then he sought and locked her gaze with his. "What are you doing?" she asked weakly.

"I'm letting you feel me." And feel him she did. The power pounding against her hand, as well as the electricity crackling between them, was enough to turn the cold stairwell into a sweltering inferno. He slowly reached his other hand out and placed it over her heart.

"I see that we still have the same effect on each other."

"But…we're not the same people anymore," she offered weakly.

"Aren't we?" he challenged. "Is Captain Crunch still your favorite cereal? When you get upset, do you still throw on your favorite Mary J. Blige CD?"

She blinked.

"Are the New York Mets still your favorite baseball team? Is yellow still your favorite color? Do you still cry when you watch *The Color Purple?*"

Tears started to burn the back of Corona's eyes. The realization that her fiancé didn't know those small things about her hit hard.

"I bet you still love Pepsi over Coke, dancing in your underwear on Saturday mornings and…me," he added, pressing her farther up against the wall.

"Wh-what?" She barely got the question out before her throat started to close up.

"I didn't see it last night. Maybe I was too blinded by jealousy, but now…I'm convinced that you're still in love with me."

She couldn't get herself to sputter out a denial right away. She helplessly watched a confident—or rather cocky—smile curl the corners of Lyfe's lips. And still, words eluded her.

"I can't believe I almost left here without getting what I came here for."

Finally finding the power to swallow the lump in her throat, she rasped, "And what's that?"

"You," he said.

There was no hiding her heart's wild pounding against his hand. In fact, she felt like she'd been completely stripped naked in that staircase, and she didn't know what to do about it.

"I don't think it even matters anymore why you ran. Maybe you were scared. Maybe you simply thought that we were just too young," he said. "It doesn't matter. All I want to know is how you feel now. At this very moment."

She squirmed. "I—I—"

"Would you like me to kiss you?" He finally moved his hand from her heart, so that he could gently brush the side of her face. "I want to kiss you. I want to see if you taste as sweet as I remember."

Corona melted. Lyfe had to withdraw his hand and wrap it around her waist so that she would remain on her feet.

"I won't kiss you unless you say that it's okay," he said, leaning in closer.

Every muscle in her body morphed into a swarm of butterflies, and she was afraid that if she opened her mouth one would fly out. But her inability to talk didn't distract Lyfe from his singular focus: her lips.

"Do you want me to kiss you, Corona Mae? Do you want to see if we still have that same magic we used to?"

A tear rolled off her thick lashes, but before it reached

her cheek, Lyfe had absorbed it on the pad of his finger. "What's this for? There's no need for tears. I just want what I've always wanted—to make you happy. And if you say that that other man makes you happy, then I'm going to step off."

Corona couldn't even think of the man he was referring to.

"So what do you want me to do?"

Overwhelmed by the heat of his body, quivering with anticipation and curiosity, she whispered, "Kiss me."

Chapter 17

The sexiest smile slid across Lyfe's lips a fraction of a second before his head descended. The two seconds it took for their mouths to connect felt more like a lifetime, but the reward was well worth the wait. That underlying sweetness she remembered was still there, but there was also so much more.

More power.

More richness.

This was not a kiss of puppy love. This was a kiss of a confident man who knew how to do manly things.

They were weightless and suspended in what felt like an alternate time and place. In his arms, she was grace and beauty…and love. Just like that. It was as if there hadn't been more than a dozen years since they'd been in each other's arms—melting from each other's kisses. At the heart…there was still a strong foundation of love.

There was no room for reason and reality at this

moment. The past didn't matter and tomorrow was just too far away for her to be concerned about. All that mattered was right here and right now.

In no time at all, she was returning his kiss with the same fierce hunger that he was trying to devour her with. When she heard a deep growl rumble from his chest, Corona felt a surge of power course through her. Her ego couldn't help but inflate at the realization that she still had power over him. She could do whatever she wanted with him, right here and right now. The question was whether she dared to take that leap.

Her mind tangled with this question until Lyfe tore his lips away from hers. He blazed a trail of fiery kisses across her jawbone and then down her long neck. Corona rasped as she sucked in some much needed oxygen. Maybe the air would help dispel her naughty thoughts.

No such luck.

Her hands splayed across his chest. Once again, she could feel his hammering heart against her palms. She was doing that to him—and she could do much more—if she dared.

Lyfe's lips grazed the magic spot at the juncture of her neck and collarbone, and suddenly she had her answer. Corona jerked his shirt up from the waist of his pants, desperate to press flesh against flesh.

Once she had given the signal, Lyfe's hand went to work as well. Suddenly the hem of her skirt flew up her firm thighs and cinched around her waist. Then his hands got busy caressing and squeezing her ass. A lethal dose of pheromones went straight to Corona's head and the whole world tilted sideways.

When she got her hands underneath his shirt, she

discovered a rippling six-pack, a V-cut hip and an astonishing broad, muscular chest that was as hard as his skin was soft.

A steady drip of honey soaked her panties. A half second later, Lyfe wrenched those to the corner of her thighs so that his fingers could dip inside. He wasted no time zeroing in on her pulsing clit, where the pads of his fingers performed a seductive twirl and dipped beneath the base.

"Ohh." Corona dropped her head all the way back, giving his hot mouth permission to now slide down the valley of her breasts.

The moment his mouth latched onto her right nipple, an unbearable ache began to radiate through her entire body. She needed him. More than she'd ever needed anything in her entire life. Her hand raked down to the waist of his pants, where she fumbled with the button and zipper for what seemed like forever. But, in truth, it just took a few seconds for her to have what she'd been searching for pulsing in the palm of her hand.

Well, hello.

There had been a few more changes to Lyfe Alton over the years. Every inch of it good. Very good.

"What do you plan to do with that, Ms. Banks?" Lyfe asked, silkily. "Tell me."

Corona could instantly think of a million things to do with him, and while she mulled those over she lazily slid her hands up and down his growing inches. She even took time to marvel at the intricate veins throbbing on its sides, and the fat mushroom head that was beginning to ooze with pre-cum.

Lyfe abandoned her breasts to pay homage to her left earlobe, where he could whisper, "I've missed you so much, Corona." He nibbled on her lower lobe. "I've missed you so very much." With a slight twist of his hips, he nudged his cock closer to her dripping pussy. "Have you missed me, too?"

"Yes," Corona answered without hesitation.

"How much?" The tip of his cock brushed against her wet lips.

"More than you'll ever know," she admitted.

Lyfe pulled his head back so that he could stare into her eyes and see the truth. When he saw what he was looking for, he slanted his mouth over hers so that he could brand her with another scorching kiss.

Corona knew better than to have sex with no condom and standing in the middle of a public staircase with her panties jacked to the side. But reason and logic continued to leak out of her brain at a steady pace.

Hiking her left leg around his trim waist and dipping her right knee was enough to ease the tip of Lyfe's dick into her honeyed walls.

Following her direction, Lyfe grabbed her other leg and pinned her to the wall. Gravity slid him in the rest of the way.

Air seeped out of Corona's lips in a slow hiss while she tried to adjust to feeling him in the center of her belly—or at least, that's how far it felt like he'd reached. Once she thought that she was ready, she locked her ankles behind his back and prepared herself for the ride of her life.

She didn't have to wait long. From the very first stroke, Corona was lost. The mere exquisiteness of their joining was enough to send twin streams of tears pouring from her closed eyes.

"Oh, baby. I've missed you so much," Lyfe moaned as he kissed away those same tears.

Corona dipped and rolled her hips, drawing him in even deeper and causing his breath to draw ragged.

"You're mine...and you'll always be mine." His words and his body continued to brand her in ways one would think impossible. "Look at me, baby," he urged.

It took several strokes for her to find the strength to flutter open her long lashes.

"I want you to know who is inside you—who has always been inside you."

Her mouth sagged into an elongated "O" as his hips grinded harder to the left.

"You'll never be rid of me, baby," Lyfe panted. "You belong to me." With that declaration, he slanted his mouth across hers and delved his hot tongue into her mouth where it danced and seduced her own.

Soon, small orgasmic quakes started trembling as far down as her toes, then they climbed toward her calves, knees and thighs. By the time the pressure started building in her clit she was squirming in his arms, trying to figure out how to prepare for something that felt like a tsunami heading her way. At long last, she just surrendered and took the force of her explosion head-on.

Corona tore her lips away and cried out. The sound magnified as it reverberated throughout the empty staircase.

"It's freezing out here!" Amanda complained, racing down 34th Street behind Melody.

"Just hurry up," Melody said, dodging patches of ice like a seasoned ballerina. "The faster we get there, the faster we can get out of the cold," she told her best friends. After her aunt had hung up on her, Melody had called her grandparents, asked what hotel they were staying at and told them that she was on her way to come see them. They were ecstatic—they only had a phone relationship with their granddaughter since her mother never wanted to return to Georgia, and her grandparents could never afford to come to New York.

But it didn't affect things too much. She usually talked to them every Sunday night, and in the last two years they had actually been able to see each other via the internet. Now that she had their hotel information, she had every intention of digging for more information about this Lyfe Alton character.

"I can't feel my legs," Carrie complained. "And I think my lashes are trying to freeze together."

"Ohmigod, you two!" Melody rolled her eyes. "Just hurry up. We're almost there."

But even a few minutes felt like a lifetime in this blistering cold. Melody didn't even care that, by the time they rushed into the lobby of the Four Seasons, she could no longer feel her face. She just made a bee-line to the elevators.

"Will you wait up," Amanda shouted. "What's the hurry?"

"I don't want Aunt Tess to leave."

"I thought you were going to see your grandparents?" Carrie said.

"I will—*but* after I talk to Aunt Tess. I know if I press hard enough she'll crack. My grandparents will just toe the line of waiting until my mother tells me about my father. They'll be too hard to crack." She pressed for the elevator again. "Why is this damn thing taking so damn long?" She jerked away. "Where's the staircase?"

"What? We're taking the stairs now?" Amanda groaned. "I'm starting to feel like we're in PE class."

"C'mon, slackers." Melody laughed as she found the staircase and rushed inside. "It'll help you warm up faster."

There was some more groaning and complaining but they continued to race behind her. They managed to jog up two flights before a strange sound reached their ears.

Melody came to a full stop. "Shh. Do you hear that?"

Huffing and puffing, the girls struggled to quiet their breathing to listen. Slowly, one by one, their mouths fell open.

"Is that what I think it is?" Amanda asked, her eyes bugging.

Carrie giggled. "Somebody is making out." She walked over to the railing and tried to glance upward.

"Stop it." Melody laughed. "What if they see you?"

"Me? They're the ones who should be embarrassed."

"I wonder who it is." Amanda said, starting to take off up the stairs.

Melody quickly grabbed her by the arm and hissed. "Get back here. What do you think you're doing?"

"I'm being nosy. What does it look like?"

"I don't think so." Melody wasn't in the mood to try and embarrass anyone, so she dragged them back out of the staircase. "We'll take the elevator."

Carrie and Amanda issued a final groan of complaint before leaving the mystery lovers alone in the staircase above them.

Lyfe roared in the sweaty crook of Corona's shoulder. He had never in his life been able to come back-to-back like this. The little devil in his head was steadily trying to convince him that he could go yet another round.

"Wait. Wait," Corona panted, clearly struggling to catch her breath.

He forced himself to hold back, but he didn't release her. He didn't think that he could ever do that again. He didn't even want to think about how close he'd come to not having this moment. How he could've easily made that flight to Atlanta with his tail tucked between his legs. This was all the proof he needed that Corona still had feelings for him; and that perhaps they could bridge whatever differences they may have had.

Hope, something he'd long given up on, pricked his heart and filled his head with wondrous possibilities. After a full minute, the reminted lovers started to ease their grip on one another as the reality of what had just transpired began to take root.

"Ohmigod. What have I done?" She pushed at his chest so that she could lower her legs. However, standing proved to be too challenging, and she slid down the wall and onto the floor.

Lyfe immediately stepped back and kneeled down next to her. "It's all right. I don't want you to panic."

"Not panic?" she said, scrambling across the floor to gather her things and cram them back into her purse.

"Whoa. Whoa. What are you doing?"

"I've got to get out of here. I have to go."

"Wait. Slow down. Let me help you." He grabbed several lipsticks and handed them back to her. "I think that we need to talk about what just happened."

"What's there to talk about? I just screwed around on my fiancé!"

Riiiiinnnng! Riiiinnnng!

Both of their heads jerked toward her cell phone, which sounded like it was miked up to a bullhorn in the acoustic staircase. On the screen popped up a picture of the very photogenic Rowan James, with his name typed above it.

"Ohmigod," Corona moaned again, while shame and embarrassment colored her entire face. "What am I going to tell him?"

"Well, first, you might want to tell him that you're having second thoughts about your wedding."

Riiiiiinnnng! Riiiinnnng!

"What?" Corona twisted up her face as she grabbed the phone, shut it off, and then crammed it back into her purse. "Who said that I was having second thoughts?"

He blinked, caught off guard. "Well, clearly what just happened—"

"What just happened was a mistake," she declared, jumping back to her feet. "It meant nothing. It changes nothing."

She couldn't have caused more damage if she'd pointed an assault weapon at him and unloaded an entire clip. Seeing the effect of her words, she quickly tried to repair some of the damage. "I'm sorry. I—I…this was just wrong." She shoved her skirt back down her legs and made a halfhearted attempt to button her blouse. "I gotta go!"

Corona took off running, even though her legs were like Jell-O.

"Corona Mae," Lyfe shouted, cramming himself back into his pants before taking off after her.

"Please, just leave me alone," Corona shouted, hearing him closing in on her.

"We need to talk!"

"There's nothing to talk about," she insisted. Knowing that she wasn't going to be able to outrun him on the staircase she shoved through the doors of the next landing and raced to find the elevator bay. As luck would have it, the door was just closing, and she managed to slip through it before Lyfe caught up.

"Corona Mae!" Lyfe thundered behind her.

The door closed. When the elevator started its descent, her entire body imploded with relief and the tears streamed down her face.

Chapter 18

"What's the room number again?" Carrie asked, scanning the hallway of the tenth floor.

"Here it is," Melody said, pointing. When she stopped in front of the door she took a second to draw in a deep breath and calm her nerves.

Sensing her nervousness, her two best friends wrapped their arms around her shoulders and gave her an encouraging squeeze.

"Don't worry," Amanda said. "We have your back."

"Yeah," Carrie said and then tossed in a wink. "We got you, girl."

"All right. Here goes." Melody lifted her hand to knock. But before she got a chance, the door swung open and an incredibly handsome giant towered above them.

"Oh, hello, ladies," he said in a hypnotic baritone.

One by one, their mouths dropped open, and their legs seemed to take root where they stood.

"Oookay." He chuckled under his breath and then struggled to squeeze by them. Once he'd gotten by, he continued to laugh to himself while he strolled down the hall.

The three teenagers' gazes followed him until he disappeared into another room.

Amanda was the first to find her voice, "Did you see him?"

Tess's voice floated toward the door. "What on earth is going on here?"

Melody turned and then watched her aunt gasp with surprise.

"Ohmigod. It's my baby!" She threw open her arms and didn't have long to wait before Melody stepped into her embrace. "I can't believe it. Look how big you are!" She pulled her niece out of her arms so she could take another look at her. "I can't believe it, you look so much like your…" She caught herself.

"Like who?" Melody seized on the opening.

"Like your mother," Tess covered.

Needless to say, they both knew *that* was a lie. No one had ever thought that Melody looked like her mother. Her skin was darker, her eyes lighter and she didn't have a clue where she had inherited her dimples from.

"I hope you don't mind me and my girlfriends just dropping by," Melody said, turning and waving her friends into the room.

"Uh, of course not," Tess said, smiling at her friends. "The more the merrier." She walked over to the door and glanced out into the hallway before shutting it.

"Soooo," Melody began. "Who was your friend?"

"Uhh…my friend?"

Melody didn't know what to make of her aunt blushing as hard as she was. "Is he your boyfriend or something?"

Tess threw out a genuine laugh. "Hardly."

And still, Melanie noted, she didn't answer the question. She cut a look over at her girlfriends, who were still feverishly fanning themselves.

"All I know is that's the kind of man I want when I grow up," Carrie said, leaning over toward Amanda. "Did you see how wide his shoulders were?"

"Forget that. What about that smile?"

Tess laughed. "All right, ladies. Get a hold on your hormones. You have plenty of time before you have to start worrying about boys."

"Boys?" Carrie volleyed. "We're talking about men. And I won't mind waiting a lifetime for someone like him."

Tess shook her head and then turned her attention back to her niece. "Sooo, how did you know where I was staying?"

"Grandma," Melody answered nonchalantly, as she shrugged off her backpack and pulled out one of her mother's diaries.

Tess groaned. "Sweetheart—"

"Aunt Tess, please. You just got to help me. I just know that this Lyfe Alton has to be my father. The timeline fits and everything."

"Honey, it's just—"

"And, please, please don't tell me to talk to Mom. She keeps saying that she'll tell me when I'm older, and I can't wait anymore."

Her aunt looked like she was weakening, but she only said, "It's just not my place to talk to you about this."

"Whatever you tell me, I swear I won't tell Mom."

"And if I don't tell you anything?"

Melody drew a deep breath. "Then I'll find him on my own."

Lyfe was convinced that he needed his head examined. It was the only logical conclusion. How many times was he going to let Corona Mae make a fool of him? After sharing something so beautiful, he was now returning to his hotel room feeling dirty and used. Hell, all that was missing to complete the humiliating experience was her tossing money in his face.

And yet, he still had hope. Was he crazy? Was he a glutton for punishment?

"No. This is what I get for listening to my brother." He punched the button for the other elevator and waited. There was no point in racing down to the lobby. He was sure that by the time he got there, Corona Mae would be long gone. No. He needed to fall back for a minute, give her a little space and then come at her another way.

Lyfe ran that plan through his head again and liked it even better the second time around. By the time his elevator arrived, a smile was carving back on to his face. As he stepped into the compartment and pushed for the tenth floor, his mind started to rerun images of the hot quickie in the stairwell.

There was so much passion in Corona's kiss and so much heat in her touch that she'd had him, once again, feeling like the seventeen-year-old kid who had been so desperate to please her. Of course there were a few major changes. He liked to think that this time he knew what the hell he was doing. But the amazing thing was that he still knew all her G-spots and had worked them accordingly.

Hell. If he could get her into a bed…or even a floor again, he would certainly show her a few new tricks. Of course, there was the voice in the back of his head screaming to remind him that she was now an engaged woman. But, while that was true, Stevie Wonder had famously crooned that all in love is fair. Lyfe was officially declaring war on Rowan James for the prize of his life.

The elevator dinged and the steel doors slid open. Lyfe took one step out before a young teenager plowed straight into him.

"Oops. I'm sorry," she said, hardly glancing up at him.

"It's no problem." He smiled and then moved out of the way so that she could catch the elevator.

"Melody, wait up!" Two other teenaged girls called out, racing down the hallway. The moment they saw him they slowed up, and two huge smiles spread over their faces.

Lyfe tipped his head. "Afternoon, ladies."

That launched them into a fit of giggles as they joined their friend in the elevator.

He even caught the exchange of, "Dag, he's cuter than the other one."

"I don't know. I think it's a draw."

The one they had called Melody rolled her eyes. "Don't you girls ever think about anything other than boys?"

Her friends looked at each other as the elevator's doors started to close and said, "No."

Lyfe chuckled. "Out of the mouths of babes."

Chapter 19

The Christmas holidays were in full swing in New York. The entire city had transformed into a magical winter wonderland with sappy Christmas songs clogging up the radios and pouring out of every store. But with every tick of the clock, Corona felt herself turning more into an Ebenezer Scrooge than a St. Nick. It wasn't just that she had to plan a great Christmas for Melody... and now her grandparents, too; but she was also running around trying to plan a wedding with her future mother-in-law, Cruella De Vil, aka Wahida James. As if that wasn't enough, she had poor Margo giving Lyfe one excuse after another of why she couldn't take his calls or return them.

After a week, she could tell that Margo was developing her own suspicions on the matter. And when Margo got suspicious, she got gossipy. It also didn't help that winter flowers were being delivered daily, signed,

"From your first and only love." At first Margo had cooed about the flowers coming from Rowan, but now it was written on her face that she knew that the flowers were being sent from the man she lied to every day.

None of this was helping her absolve herself of the guilt that accumulated daily for cheating on her fiancé. She doubted that anything could help her with that. Every time Rowan called telling her about his long grueling hours or how the director didn't know his head from a hole on the wall, the world crashed down on Corona's shoulders.

I have to tell him. However, every time that thought whispered from the back of her head it was quickly crowded out by counter thoughts of how much the confession would destroy Rowan. After all, his last fiancé had had an affair on him.

But it's not an affair. It was...an incident—a fifteen-minute incident.

She groaned. That sounded awful, even to her ears.

"Ms. Banks, are you there?"

"Uh, what?" She'd forgotten that she was even on the phone with Universal Media Studios. "Oh, I'm sorry about that, Ted. I just spilled some coffee on my desk. I got a little distracted," she lied.

"Not a problem." The producer chuckled. "I did that at least three times this morning myself." He went back over the list of actors that he would be keeping for the next season of his television show.

This time she jotted it down, because the way her mind was working lately she wasn't going to remember the list the moment they hung up.

"By the way, I hope my invitation to the wedding doesn't get lost in the mail," Ted joked. "I can't believe that you're actually going to marry some other guy—an actor, no less. All this time, I thought that I was making progress," he said.

Corona tried to laugh, but it sounded stiff and flat to her own ears.

"Are you excited?"

It was a simple and legitimate question; however, Corona's answer was anything but. "It's…it's a lot of planning…and work. You know, marriage isn't something that one should take on lightly. I mean, I have a daughter. Her…concerns should be taken into account. You know what I mean? Plus, it's not like I still have feelings for…someone else. That was in the past. A long time ago. One can never just go back to how something was after all this time. Can they? One has to move on. Put one foot in front of the other and just let go. Right?"

There was a long silence over the phone while Corona mentally reviewed that lovely word vomit that she had just spit out.

"Okay, then, uhm," Ted said, "I guess that I'll just see you at the wedding."

"Yes!" She injected enthusiastically. "I can't wait to see you there." She quickly hung up the phone and then plopped her head into her hands. "All right, girl. Pull it together."

Riiiiiinnnng!

She lifted her head and snatched up the phone before reading the Caller ID screen. "Yeah."

"Yeah?" Lyfe chuckled over the line. "Is that how the big movers and shakers answer the phone in this city?"

"Lyfe?" She jumped out of her seat and twisted her neck to see out the side-glass paneling next to her door. Margo was nowhere to be seen.

"Well, I guess at this point I should be happy that you even remember my name."

Corona drew a deep breath, but it didn't do anything to stop the heat simmering in her core. "Of course, I remember your name." She glanced around the room. "You're the man who has turned my office into a flower shop."

"Aww. So you did get them," he said. "I was beginning to think the little man at the florist was lying to me. I didn't get a thank-you call from you."

Corona drew a deep breath while searching for the courage to say what she needed to say. "You didn't get a call because I didn't have any intentions of calling you."

"Ouch. You really do know how to hurt a guy," he said, but he didn't sound the least bit hurt at all.

Now that she'd gotten what she considered to be the hard part out, Corona continued, "Look, Lyfe, I told you at the hotel that...what happened—"

"You mean my making love to you up against a wall?"

An instant image flashed inside her head. "I—uhm, yes. That incident was...regrettable."

"Incident? Regrettable?" Lyfe paused, and then his laughter rumbled through the phone line.

The warmth that Corona was experiencing was quickly morphing into a heat wave. Not only did Lyfe have a face and body that any of her male runway models would die for, but he had a voice that could make a woman's panties melt over the phone.

"Are those the words you used to explain to your fiancé what happened between us?"

Corona dropped back down into her chair, and, this time, she really did knock over her coffee. "Oh, dammit."

"Careful. That's hot stuff," Lyfe said.

"Shh. I know it. Don't you think…" She stopped just as she was about to reach for a box of Kleenex on the corner of her desk. "Wait. How do you know what just happened?"

Her office door pushed open and Lyfe filled up the doorway. "Because I can see you."

"What are you doing here?" she still asked into the phone, even though she was looking dead at him.

He continued talking into the phone as well. "Well, I figured that since you wouldn't call me back, I would come by and see you."

Corona shook her head even as he stepped farther into her office. "You shouldn't have come here."

He cocked his head and took his time drinking her in. "No. I should've followed you to New York a long time ago." He finally made it over to her desk, leaned one hip on the edge and then reached over and gently removed the phone from her hands. When he hung it up, he punched the Do Not Disturb button and then pocketed his own phone.

"Once I got up here, I should have made you tell me to my face why you left." He locked gazes with her. "I should have made you look me in the eye and tell me that you didn't love me anymore and that you didn't want to have a future with me—or have my children."

Corona bounced out of her chair like a hot Pop-Tart. "You have to go."

"Wait." Lyfe's hand snaked out and caught her around the wrist.

"No," she snapped, jerking her hand free. "You're not funny."

At the word *"no,"* Lyfe eased back and held up both

hands in surrender. "Hey, calm down. I'm not the type of man that's going to force you to do something that you don't want to do. I love children, but if you don't want to have any…"

"What?" Corona stepped back again and studied his face. *He doesn't know. How is it possible that he doesn't know?*

"Just like I wasn't the one who initiated our last… regrettable incident." He cocked his head again and hit her with a smile that she remembered from his high school football days. For a moment, she felt the urge to pump her fists like pom-poms, like she had in the good ol' days.

Lyfe lowered his hands. "You do remember asking me to kiss you in that stairwell, don't you?"

"That was—"

"And you do remember how fast you melted in my arms, don't you?" He stood up from the desk and moved toward her.

At the sudden lack of oxygen, Corona stepped back and then heard herself beg, "Please."

"Don't worry," he said, his voice dropping to a lower register. "I'm only going to do what you ask me to do."

Her head jerked up. "Then leave. Go back home to Atlanta."

"Well…anything but that," he amended, holding on to that same cocky smile. "See…your beautiful lips say leave, but, when I kissed you, those same lips begged me to stay. I wonder what else they'll say when I get you the way that I want you."

She bravely took another step back. "That's never going to happen."

He took another step and erased the small distance between them. "Don't you know to never say never?"

"Lyfe, I'm engaged."

"Engagements can be broken. You taught me that."

She opened her mouth, but no words came out. What could she say to that?

"Tell you what. I'm going to cut you a break," Lyfe said, folding his arms. "You want me to leave? Go back to Atlanta and permanently stay out of your life? There's only one way that I'll agree to do it."

Corona also folded her arms. "I'm listening."

"One date."

"No." She shook her head, seeing the trap for what it was.

"Then I guess I'll be sticking around. You do remember that your fiancé invited me to be one of his groomsmen."

"That was when he thought you were marrying my sister."

"I still might. If she buys me the right ring."

"You're not funny."

He cocked his head the other way. "Actually, I'm hilarious. I used to make you laugh until milk squirted out of your nose."

She didn't mean to, but she smiled.

"Ah. There's my Corona Mae." Without warning, he reached out and pulled her into his arms. "God. How I've missed you."

There was one solitary voice in the back of her head that told her to push her way out of his arms, but damn if she could get herself to do it.

"What's with this whole Chloe thing, anyway?"

"It's—just more professional sounding. It's not…"

"Country?"

Another smile. "Something like that."

"Well, I love Corona Mae." He reached up and brushed her hair away from her face. "Always have—always will."

She should have seen the kiss coming. But, then again, maybe she did and chose to do nothing about it. The next thing she knew, she was being swept away in a kiss that made her feel seventeen again. In her head, visions of them laughing on a baseball field, posing for junior prom and even sneaking away to go skinny dipping at old Robin Lake flashed in her head. This man had been more than just her first lover, he'd been her best friend.

When the kiss ended, he pulled back and smiled tenderly at her. "One date."

She swallowed.

Lyfe continued, "If by the end of it, you still want me out of your life forever, I'll go." He cupped her face. "But if it goes the way I think it will, you'll break your engagement and marry me."

Chapter 20

Lyfe couldn't believe that Corona Mae hadn't tried to cancel on him. Either she meant to try to outfox him so she could get rid of him, or she was privately hoping that the night would go according to his plans.

He was taking her to the exclusive Per Se restaurant at the Time Warner Center complex. From everything he'd heard about the place it had the perfect balance of intimacy and understated luxury. But he wished that she would've allowed him to pick her up instead of just meeting him at the restaurant. Then again, it was understood that as hard as he was going to try to seduce her, she was likely going to do all she could to prevent it from happening.

When he arrived at the restaurant, he couldn't believe that he actually had butterflies—just like he had when he'd arrived at her house to take her to junior prom. He must've waited twenty minutes downstairs, watching her father while he cleaned his gun. He had sweated so much that her father ended up asking him whether he had a sweat gland problem.

Now, here he was; waiting with those same butterflies. But after twenty minutes of waiting, he started to wonder whether he'd been stood up. Lyfe pulled out his cell phone at least a dozen times, imagining he heard it ring or double checking the number of bars showing.

Just when he was about to give up hope, Corona Mae breezed into the restaurant, a striking figure in a snow-white coat.

"There you are," he said, sounding and feeling relieved. "I was beginning to think that you'd changed your mind."

"No. A deal is a deal."

"Well. Let's see about our table, shall we?" he asked, helping her slip out of her coat. Beneath it was a matching white wrap-dress that hugged her curves as much as he wanted to tonight. "You look gorgeous."

"Thank you," she said, smiling. "You clean up rather well yourself."

Lyfe offered her his arm and then led her to the hostess. Within seconds they were escorted to a table that gave them a breathtaking, wintry view of Central Park. After their drink orders were taken a surprising awkward silence enveloped them.

"It's kind of strange, huh?" he said. "Our first official date as grown-ups." When she smiled, he relaxed.

"Yeah. It is sort of strange." She reached for her glass of water and they both spotted how badly her hand was trembling.

"Wow. I can't remember a time when I made *you* nervous."

"You're joking, right? How about the time when you convinced me to egg and toilet paper Mr. Henderson's house because of a silly bet you made with your brother Dorian? Or the first time we went skinny dipping at Robin Lake and your brothers Ace and Hennessey came and stole our clothes?"

Lyfe laughed.

"And then there was that first time that we..." Corona Mae caught herself.

"The first time we made love?" he asked.

Their waiter appeared and asked for their drink orders.

Despite hating the guy's timing, Lyfe quickly selected them a cabernet sauvignon and tried to return to their discussion. "Does that night hold fond memories for you?" he asked.

Corona's cheeks darkened. "You know it does."

He smiled. "Well, it's not like we had much discussion about it. The next day, we were engaged and then—"

"Yes. Yes. I remember," she said, reaching for her water glass again.

"Why did you leave?" he asked, before he could stop himself. He'd prepped himself not to ask that question, and even told himself in the mirror that he no longer cared and that he just wanted to leave it in the past and start anew. But, at the heart of it, he still needed and wanted an answer.

Corona tugged in a deep breath and then met his steady gaze. "I thought...to prevent us from making a big mistake."

Lyfe blinked. Her answer hurt more than he thought it would. "A mistake?"

She nodded. "We were just kids. Too young to be strapped down by some archaic ideology that dictated that what we had done—what we had shared—had somehow brought shame to the family name. You get married because you're in love."

"We were in love," he said. "At least I was in love."

Her smile returned. "So was I…but at seventeen it's just not enough. We hadn't finished high school, or gone to college, or even discovered who we really were. I couldn't get my father to listen, and my mother didn't seem like she wanted to intercede so…"

"You just left. Without even a note?" Lyfe tried to keep the hurt out of his voice, but he was failing miserably.

Tears glistened in Corona's eyes. "If I left a note at that time, you would've come after me. You would've tried to convince me that life with you working on the farm and me in my mother's hair salon would've been just fine."

"It would've been."

"For a while, yes. But that wasn't who we were or even what we wanted to be—and it wasn't up to my father to make that decision for us. I love him and we still have a ways to go to heal that hurt, but…he was wrong."

Lyfe nodded while he let her words sink in. So far, he couldn't disagree with anything she'd said. He would've settled for the life of a farmer instead of trying his luck and making it as an architect; and she would've never had an opportunity to become a hotshot agent in New York.

"I see your point," he finally said. "Don't mean that it doesn't still hurt like hell."

"I'm sorry," she whispered and again reached for her water. *Tell him now!* She almost choked when the voice in the back of her head screamed for her to act. It was a great opening for her bring up his daughter, but she hadn't decided on the right wording to tell him that he had a thirteen-year-old daughter. It wasn't something that you just blurted out before you even had a chance to order dinner.

The waiter returned with their wine. While he and Lyfe went through the whole ritual of showing the label and taste testing, she was mentally having a minor heart attack.

"Are you ready to place your order?"

"May I?" Lyfe asked.

"Sure. Go ahead."

"I think we'd like to start off with your signature Pearls and Oysters…"

Corona tuned out the ordering and returned to strategizing how to drop the incredible bombshell on him. And when was the right moment for that sort of thing, during dinner or dessert? Or maybe it was when they took a leisurely stroll around Rockefeller Center? Would he yell, scream, tell her how much he hated her?

"Corona, are you all right?"

She jerked herself out of her private thoughts again. "Yeah. I'm fine."

He thanked the waiter and sent him away. "I still can't get over the fact that we're actually doing this. I think our first date when we were kids was at the Hollywood Roller Rink. You remember that?"

"Do I remember? You spent half the night making me fall because you didn't know how to balance yourself on wheels. I had more bruises that night than if I'd played in a yearlong dodge ball competition."

Lyfe rocked back with a hearty laugh. "You? I broke my tailbone that night. I had to sit on a rubber donut for six months. You have no idea the kind of hell my brothers put me through for that one. They'd bring me rubber duckies and pacifiers, as if I was some kind of baby."

"Your brothers are a riot."

"They're something."

"Any of them married?"

"Can't think of a woman crazy enough to take one of them."

"Do they still have that same three-month rule?"

"I plead the fifth," he said, shaking his head.

"You didn't take up that rule, did you?"

"Who me? Nah. I could never find another woman who could…"

Take your place.

He didn't say it, but they both heard it nonetheless.

By the time their meal arrived, they had relaxed and were chitchatting about old times. After a while, it even started to feel like old times.

Corona melted each time his dimple winked at her or his intense gaze turned up the heat in the restaurant by several degrees. Before they knew it, their meals were finished and they had agreed to share a dessert. It felt wonderful to have her best friend back and to hear about his days in college and his years building a solid career.

"I have to tell you that I think the boys at the office are getting nervous. I've been in New York for a while. They're not believing that I'm not being poached by one the big firms here."

"You could probably do well here," she said.

"Would you like having me here in New York?"

The question caught her off guard. "I'd want you to do whatever would make you happy."

"And what if I told you that you would make me very happy?"

"Lyfe—"

"Corona, I'm serious." He reached across the table and claimed her hand. "Why are we playing games here? I can look at you and tell that we're both feeling the same thing. It's in your eyes and your body language. You want me as much as I want you. I don't know how long you've been dating this...actor—but I know that it can't possibly have the same depth and fire that has *always* existed between the two of us."

It was true, but as she fixed her mouth to deny it, he gave her a look that said *"don't even try it."*

"Corona Mae, look me in my eyes and tell me that we don't belong together."

She tried, she honestly did; but she couldn't get the words out.

"I knew it."

"It's just not about us anymore."

"Your fiancé," he said.

"There's him and—"

"You just told me not too long ago that you only get married because you love someone."

"I know, but—"

"Well, do you love him?" He squeezed her hand. "As much as you love me?"

"I—I—"

"Look. Don't answer that right now. I have something else planned for us."

"I'm not going back to your hotel."

Lyfe twisted up his face. "I don't recall inviting you."

Corona jerked back and blinked in surprise. "Oh. Well. I thought—"

"Please. Get your mind out of the gutter." He shook his head and signaled the waiter for the check while Corona's face blazed with embarrassment. Thirty minutes later, Lyfe was shelling out for two tickets at the Rockefeller Center Ice Rink.

"You really want to try your hand at skating again?" Corona laughed.

"Hey, a few things have changed over the years," he said, puffing up his chest. "I can do this."

"Uhm, no. Mountains don't skate and that's exactly what you're going to look like if you put those damn things on."

"Aw. Is this concern for my well-being? Does that mean that you still have feelings for your old boyfriend after all?"

"I'm concerned about all these innocent bystanders who have no idea what's coming."

He waved off her comments. "You'll see."

"All right. A hard head makes a soft ass," she warned. A half second later, he stepped out on the ice and hit the ice hard.

"Oooh." Corona winced, shaking her head. "That looks like it hurt."

"Oh, damn. I think I broke my tailbone again."

Corona roared with laughter.

"Hey, Melody. Isn't that your mother over there?" Amanda asked, pointing across the ice rink.

Melody turned her head and saw her mother standing over some mountain of a guy, laughing her head off. "Yeah. I think so."

"I thought you said that she had some all-night business thing she had to do?" Carrie added, folding her arms. "Doesn't that guy look familiar?"

Melody took a second look at the man who was struggling to get back onto his feet, only to slam back down onto the ice. The three of them jumped and winced at the hard fall.

"Ouch."

"Damn," Amanda said, shaking her head again. "I don't think I've seen anybody that awful out here. Either he's going to need a doctor in a few minutes or he's going to crack the entire ice rink. Ooooh."

He fell again.

Her mother's laughter rang out so clear that it was infectious. "I wonder who that guy is," Melody said to herself more than her friends.

"I don't know, but he definitely doesn't look like your future stepfather. Heck, I don't think I've ever seen your mother look that happy around Rowan."

"Me either," Melody said.

"Hey, we better go if we're going to catch that show," Carrie reminded them.

"All right. I'm coming," Melody said, but didn't move.

"C'mon," Amanda grabbed her best friend by the arm. "I'm sure your mother doesn't need a chaperone."

"I'm not too sure about that," Melody said, but allowed herself to be dragged along.

After forty minutes of strenuous work, Corona had finally achieved the singular goal of getting Lyfe to stand perfectly balanced on the ice. Standing, not skating. And to be honest about her handiwork, it still looked like a good stiff wind would blow him back over.

"I got it. I got it," Lyfe boasted as if he was four years old.

"Now just think of your skates like a pair of skis. You want to keep them parallel."

"Skis. All right. Got it."

Corona took a deep breath while weighing whether he was really ready for the next step. "All right. Now I want you to use your dominant foot and gently push yourself forward."

"Just…push," he repeated several times before he actually attempted it. The next thing she knew, he was wobbling, his hands were doing the whole helicopter thing, and he was going down.

And she was going down with him.

"Oooof!" Lyfe's eyes bulged as she landed on top of him, knocking what little air he had left out of his body.

Once they were able to catch their breath again, they were laughing. When they stopped, their faces and lips were just inches apart. From there, gravity took care of the rest.

Corona's head spun until she was dizzy with desire. His touch. His taste. She simply couldn't get enough. He tasted like hope and promise and a destiny unfulfilled. When their lips pulled apart, Lyfe stared lovingly into her eyes.

"Come back to my hotel."

Chapter 21

This is wrong.

But despite that realization, Corona couldn't stop herself from touching and kissing Lyfe as they stumbled into the elevator of the Four Seasons. On one hand, she was being completely driven by an unquenchable lust and, on the other, she felt more love radiating from this man than she had known in her entire lifetime. His spirit and essence infused her own and had her feeling like she was floating on clouds of ecstasy.

Stop. It's not too late to stop.

But it *was* too late. She wouldn't have been able to pull herself away from this man even if her soul was on the line. She heard a bell and they tumbled out onto his floor, still caressing and clawing at each other's clothes. There could've been other people in the hallway, but neither of them cared. Their concentration was only on each other, except for the two seconds it took for Lyfe to inject his card key into the lock.

They spilled into the room, where the only light came from the winter's moon cascading through the sheer curtains. Shoes were kicked off and sent flying into the air as hands tried to re-familiarize themselves with each other's body.

With one quick pull to the ties on her wrap dress, Lyfe was treated to the sight of her dangerous curves encased in black lace. One look at her in the silvery moonlight and Lyfe's heart went into overdrive. He was certain that there was no more beautiful sight on earth.

He quickly stilled Corona's hands, which had been jerking open his pants, and lifted them and pinned them over her head. "Whoa, whoa, sweetheart," he whispered against her ear. "Let's slow down. I want us to take our time." Lyfe brushed a long kiss across her jawline. "Like we did our first time."

Corona squirmed beneath him as if she couldn't take a slower pace. It was like she was on fire and would be reduced to ashes if he didn't give her what she needed. And though he liked the seductive sight of her moaning and writhing, he refused to be deterred from his plans for her tonight.

"Trust me, baby. You're going to love this." He continued sweeping kisses down her long neck and then down the center of her body. He was certain that she would remember this move from their first time together; but, tonight, he wouldn't get distracted by suckling on her nipples. Instead, he and his roaming tongue continued to sink lower down her body with a different destination.

Corona sighed and quivered when she felt Lyfe's large

hands peel down her La Perla panties. At the feel of the delicate fabric sliding off her hips and then gliding down her legs, she held her breath in anxious anticipation.

"Oh! Nice." He chuckled lightly and then brushed a kiss against her hairless pussy.

Her quivering increased at the touch of his lips; but as she felt his tongue sliding inside and stealing her honey, the air in her lungs escaped in a long, winding hiss.

"Hmmm," Lyfe moaned, urging her legs to open east and west. From there, he opened her brown lips and revealed her glistening pink pearl. "Baby, you're so damn beautiful," he whispered before leaning in and gulping her clit.

Corona's eyes bulged as she attempted to sit straight up.

But Lyfe's hands stretched over his head and pressed her back down. Now that her lungs had been depleted of air, Corona had a hard time getting oxygen back into them. Lyfe had turned into a Tasmanian devil between her legs. Somehow he managed to slurp and tongue box her clit silly.

The pleasure was so intense that Corona tried to close her legs and push his head away, but he made it clear that none of that was going to happen until he got what he was waiting for. Two seconds later, she cried out and then grabbed fistfuls of the bedding and pulled it to her mouth so that she could bite into something—anything. It wasn't long before a second cry filled the room.

"Please. Please. I can't breathe."

Lyfe smiled and finally showed mercy. He released her pink pearl, but he still cleaned up the juices that ran down her leg. "How do you feel, baby?" he asked.

"Oh, my God. That was amazing," she panted.

"Well. You haven't seen nothing yet, baby." He rained kisses against her flat belly. "We have a lot of time to make up for. Years, in fact." He climbed off the bed and quickly stripped out of his remaining clothing.

Corona watched him through the long strands of her lashes. She couldn't convince herself that what was happening was real and not some lifelong dream. She was absolutely hypnotized by his muscles in the silvery moonlight. But having barely survived their sexual appetizer, she couldn't help but wonder what her chances were of getting through the full meal.

Turned out, she didn't have a damn thing to worry about. As he returned to the bed, he eased on top of her and kept whispering how beautiful she was and how wonderful her skin felt pressed against his.

He entered her in the middle of moaning her name, and he found her honey walls to be the perfect fit. For the first few precious seconds, he couldn't get himself to move for fear of becoming a one-minute brother. He vaguely remembered her having that effect on him the first time they joined their bodies. Surely the stakes were higher this time. Coming too soon or crying were still considered big no-no's, and for good reason.

Once he was able to gather control of himself, he started off with small strokes. He closed his eyes and then buried his head in the crook of her neck while her body continued to perform its magic over him.

Corona slid her hands up his broad back and, before long, she was gripping his shoulders and rolling her hips. After a while, their bodies rocked together in a melodious and hypnotic rhythm. A babble of words tumbled out of Corona's mouth as she found herself climbing higher among the clouds. If she could have her way, she would never come down.

So exquisite was his slow, deep stroking that tears gathered behind her closed eyes while the sound of her racing heart filled her ears. Their lips found each other's again; but their hunger for each other kept growing with every beat of their hearts.

He is your destiny.

The moment that thought floated across Corona's brain, it felt like it was a true declarative statement and not just her heart's whimsical fantasy.

And as if he'd just heard her private thoughts, Lyfe started chanting against her ear, "You belong to me. You will always belong to me."

Her toes tingled. Then it was her knees and calves. Before long, that familiar, sweet pressure started to build in her center.

Lyfe's intimate chant morphed into low guttural growls for the Almighty. Corona's muscles tightened into a smooth sheath, causing stars to start dancing before his eyes. Heaven was just a few strokes away. He could feel it. Taste it.

"You coming, baby?" he asked, not wanting to take this celestial journey without her.

Corona moaned, groaned and sighed—but she was incapable of answering him. However, her nails were slowly sinking into his body as her orgasm drew closer and closer. Before they knew it, they were crying out together. Their bodies, as well as the bed, trembled and shook as if the room was experiencing a major earthquake.

Afterward, sweaty and out of breath, they clung to each other.

"I love you, Corona Mae Banks. I always have and I always will."

I love you, too, Lyfe Alton. I always have and I always will. Instead of saying those words, she turned her head and looked at the large diamond ring still nestled on her finger.

Chapter 22

The next day passed by in a blur. Apparently, Corona had agreed to white hydrangeas and soft ranunculuses for the wedding. The original color scheme had been changed from burgundy and emerald to navy and silver because Wahida insisted that navy was Rowan's favorite color. And another seventy family and friends of her future mother-in-law just *had* to be added to the wedding list.

It got to the point that Corona just gave up arguing with the woman. She nodded to whatever she and the wedding planner put in front of her. There was only one thing on her mind: Lyfe Alton.

And then there was Rowan. She had tried to call him several times that morning and had left several messages. She needed to talk to him…so she could call off the wedding. But, until then, she felt an obligation to go through the motions. That meant she had to put up with these previously scheduled wedding planning appointments and put a smile on her face.

But there were other issues. Lyfe still didn't know about Melody.

"Chloe," Wahida shrilled. "Are you listening?"

"Huh? What?" She glanced around and noticed that she was still sitting in the cake shop with a table full of samples.

"Silly girl." Wahida rolled her eyes. "Well, which one do you like?"

Corona blinked and glanced over the table. Hell, she barely remembered tasting any of them. "The…red velvet was good," she guessed.

"Yes. It was nice…but what did you think about the coconut? We could have the chocolate sauce off to the side and—"

"I don't like coconut."

"Oh. But it's Rowan's favorite."

Corona gritted her teeth. "I. Don't. Like. Coconut."

"Yes, dear, but—"

"Damn it. No coconut!"

Wahida leaned back and put her hand over her heart. "I heard you, dear. All of New York heard you. There's no need to shout."

"You know what?" Corona jumped up, knocking her chair backward. "I have to get out of here." She grabbed her coat and her purse and raced for the door. "I'm sorry," she said as she breezed past the baker. She was certain that everyone in the shop thought that she would be the perfect candidate for the show *Bridezillas,* but she didn't care. She gulped down as much of the wintry air as she could stand.

After a full minute she calmed down. "What are you

doing, Corona Mae?" *You're planning to marry one guy while waiting anxiously to go on a date with another,* the voice in the back of her head answered. Hearing her own internal interpretation made her feel worse. "I got to get out of this date." *Then Lyfe will come to the wedding.* "Grrrr. I should kill Tess and get it over with. It's not like she hasn't had it coming for a while."

She thought about it some more and concluded that, yes, killing her sister would definitely help her feel better. Just when her impromptu stroll through New York's busy streets was becoming productive, her cell phone rang.

"Of course." She scooped her cell phone out of her jacket pocket and saw Melody's name and picture. "Hello, sweetheart."

"Mom, where are you?"

"I'm at, uhm...Times Square."

"Did you forget your appointment at Cymbeline's? Me and Grandma are waiting for you to try on dresses."

"Ohmigod." She had forgotten.

"Your driver said that you bolted out of the cake place, and he doesn't know where you went."

"I'm, uhm...on my way, sweetheart. See you in a few." She disconnected the call and rushed to the edge of the sidewalk. "Taxi!"

Twenty minutes later, Corona arrived like a hurricane at the sleek showcase room in the heart in Chelsea.

"Ah. You must be Ms. Banks," an elegant woman dressed in all black said, approaching with an outstretched hand. "I'm Gabby, and I'll be your fashion stylist today."

"Yes. I am. I'm so sorry to have kept everyone waiting. I don't know what possessed me to sign off on doing cake tasting and gown shopping on the same day."

"I completely understand. This is a very busy time for you right now. If you'd follow me, your party is waiting for you in the back."

"Thank you." Corona pulled in another deep breath and then followed her stylist to the back.

"There she is," her mother said, setting down her delicate flute of champagne and coming over to give her a huge hug. "We were really worried about you."

Tess lowered a magazine while Melody pulled the earbuds of her iPod out. She took one look at her mother's face and quickly grew concerned.

"Momma, are you all right?"

"Yeah, sure." She glanced around to see about a dozen women showcasing a variety of wedding dresses. "It's just that…" She huffed out a long breath. "It's kind of hot and stuffy in here, don't you think?" Corona fanned herself.

Her mother, Tess, and Melody all exchanged looks.

"No? Oh." She glanced around again at the smiles and the yards of silk and lace. "Maybe I just need something to drink. Maybe I just got hot running around."

Melody's frown deepened. "It's like four degrees outside, Mom."

Corona glanced up, but when she saw her daughter's steady gaze that looked so much like her father's, she quickly looked away. "Oh…yeah."

"How about some champagne?" Gabby asked, reappearing with a small tray.

"Thanks," Corona said, grabbing the glass and slamming it back almost in the same motion.

"Ooookay," Tess said, tossing her magazine onto the

coffee table. "Things look like they're getting a little more interesting."

"I think Melody is right," her mother said. "You don't look so good." She reached for her daughter and then placed the back of her hand against her forehead. "You're not running a fever, but you do look pale."

"I'm fine," Corona said and set her empty glass back on the tray. She turned to Gabby and said, "I'm going to need another one of those."

"Alrighty. Coming right up."

It actually took three drinks before Corona was ready to take a look at the dresses that she had described during her phone consultation. But the moment she was zipped into a strapless, mermaid gown with a pleated bodice, all Corona could see in the mirror was the yards of fabric of her mother's old gown with the million buttons.

Suddenly, she couldn't breathe. The dress felt like it was slowly suffocating her. "Get it off," she panted, tugging at the bodice. "Please, help me get it off."

Tess and her mother's eyes bugged.

"Please, hurry," Corona panicked. A second later, there was a loud rip from the dress, but she didn't care. She grew more frantic and began clawing at the zipper.

"Alright, baby. Calm down," her mother said, trying to get to the tiny button.

Corona dropped to her knees. "Please, please. Hurry."

"Momma?" Melody rushed over and pulled her mother's head up against her chest. "It's all right. It's okay."

At last, her mother and Tess worked the zipper down and then raked the gown off her body.

"My God," Gabby said, looking too shocked to process what had just happened.

Unable to answer, Corona busted into tears.

"Shhh. Mommy, it's okay," Melody said. She rocked her mother back and forth as her tears drenched her Christmas sweater. "It's okay."

Hours later, Corona woke up in her bed with her daughter curled up next to her. Confused, she tried to remember why and how she got there; but the effort brought on a serious migraine. Pushing herself up, she looked over at her sleeping daughter again. A smile touched her lips, and she reflected on how it'd been just the two of them for so long.

You have to tell her about her father.

The moment the thought snaked across her head, another wave of tears blurred her vision. She had put off this day for as long as she could—and she was no better prepared to talk to Melody about her father than when Melody had been in kindergarten, drawing her family tree.

What will she say? What will she do?

Knowing Melody, she'd want to meet him. *But what will he say?*

More tears skipped down her face as she tried to imagine Lyfe's reaction. The one emotion she knew he would feel would be hurt. It might even destroy him. A mountain grew in the center of her throat.

"I'm a horrible person," she choked out. Even as more tears poured down her face, she leaned over and pressed a kiss against her daughter's forehead. She turned and climbed out of bed. In the bathroom, she found her bottle of Excedrin and downed two pills.

After that, she was left to just stare at her reflection in the mirror. Her hair pointed in every direction, and her eyes were swollen from hours of crying. "You know what you have to do." She closed her eyes and pulled in another breath. This time there wouldn't be any chance of packing up her things and flying to another city. It was time to face the music.

Sighing, Corona turned and walked out of the bathroom. She remained quiet enough to tiptoe out, grab the cordless phone and creep into the living room. Surprisingly, she found her father crashed on the sofa. She really must've passed out. Spotting his jacket draped over a chair, Corona grabbed it and then tiptoed out onto her private terrace.

Once there, the below zero chill had her tugging her father's coat tighter across her body. She numbly dialed a number. While the phone rang, her heart abandoned its cozy spot inside her chest and decided to take up residency inside her throat. But the call wasn't picked up, and she was forced to leave a message.

"Hello, Rowan. This is uhm, Coro—I mean Chloe. Forgive me, but I've had a very long day and I'm currently freezing my butt off out here on my terrace." She swallowed and then tried to get to her point. "Look, I really need to talk to you—" *And I can't break up with you over the phone.* "—so, please, give me a call as soon as you get this message. All right. 'Bye." She disconnected the call but continued to stand outside, while the cold wind crystallized the few tears that tried to slide down her face.

Chapter 23

For two days, Lyfe was on top of the world. After their wonderful night together, he literally couldn't stop himself from whistling periodically throughout the day. He was so confident that he'd won the love of his life back that he'd begun researching some possible architecture firms in the big city. As far as he could tell, his prospects were looking pretty good.

"Don't forget that you have me to thank," Hennessey said over his cell's speaker. "If it wasn't for me you would've ran back here with your tail tucked between your legs."

"You mean I have Tess to thank, don't you?" Lyfe countered, even though he knew that his brother would never admit that she had been the one ultimately pulling the strings on this hook up.

"There you go again—doubting my sincere concern for your pathetic love life."

"Yeah, that makes two of us," Royce piped up. "I've been cheering from the invisible sidelines. Since you never mastered the art of being a player, I guess this Romeo and Juliet thing you got going is the next best thing."

"Make that three," Ace rumbled over the line.

"All right, all right," Lyfe cut them off before the rest of his brothers got a turn. "You've made your point, and you're all a bunch of liars—but I love you anyway."

They cracked up, sounding like a group of giants on the other end of the phone.

"Well, I got to go. I have to get things ready for this evening. I'll call you later and tell you when me and your future sister-in-law will be headed back to Atlanta."

"Damn," Hennessey said. "Somebody is cocky."

"No." Lyfe said. "Someone is in love again." He ended the call just as room service was arriving with his breakfast. He smiled extra big when he let the server into the room and tipped extra big as he exited. However, his good mood didn't last long when he reached for his newspaper and saw Rowan James's picture at the top. Peeling the paper open to the Life section, he saw the headline: ROWAN JAMES AND THE FOXX RECONCILE.

Beneath the heading was a picture of the two actors, caught making out in a bar. "Oh! This doesn't look good."

Corona sat in the center of the bed with her morning paper spread out before her and K. D. Hardaway on the television talking in her sister-girlfriend voice.

"The stars are finally realigned as Hollywood's fa-

vorite couple, Rowan James and Danica Foxx, were caught partying at all hours of the night and making out at a popular pub here in London. The hot couple is currently on location for their next film and, according to the cast and crew, the fire has been reignited from the moment the two arrived on the set. It looks like one Christmas wedding won't be happening this year!"

"Momma, turn that off," Melody said, rushing into the room with a mug of coffee. "You don't need to be watching that stuff." She quickly handed over the coffee and then snatched up the remote to turn off the TV.

"It's okay, sweetheart," Corona said, shaking her head. At least now she knew why he hadn't been returning any of her calls.

"It's *not* okay," Melody countered, frowning. "I never liked that guy."

"So I heard," Corona said, tugging in a deep breath and discovering that she really was okay with this latest development. In fact, she kept waiting for a stabbing pain or a crushing blow to hit her; but all she really felt was relief.

"Does this mean that you won't be getting married?" Melody asked.

"No, honey. I'm not getting married."

"At least not to that creep," Tess said, walking into the room with a tray of pancakes that their mother had just cooked up for her. Pancakes were always meant to make everything better.

"C'mon, Tess. He wasn't a creep. It just…wasn't meant to be. Better for us to know now than…later."

"Amen to that," her sister said. "Or I would've had to fly to London and snatch that heifer baldheaded."

Melody giggled.

"Aww. Smiles and laughter," her mother said, strolling into the bedroom. "I see that my 'Feel Better Pancakes' haven't lost their special magic."

"They sure haven't, Momma." She sliced into the syrupy, golden cakes and crammed a whole forkful into her mouth. It felt good to have her family around her. She liked the old familiar sense of home. "I'm sorry I haven't been back to Thomason," she blurted out.

Her mother's eyes grew moist. "It's okay, Corona Mae." She leaned over and pressed a kiss against her forehead.

"No, it's not, Momma. I was being selfish and stubborn and..."

"Scared," her mother filled in. "Honey, you're not the only one who has made mistakes, you know. What seems like the right thing doesn't always turn out to be so. Our hearts and our heads get us so confused sometimes that you got to learn how to forgive yourself when you listen to the wrong voice at the wrong time."

Corona smiled. "Thanks, Mom."

"You're welcome. Now eat your breakfast." She winked and then nearly tripped over her granddaughter's book bag. "Melody, sweetheart. Pick up your things and take them to your room."

"Yes, ma'am." She bent over and picked up her bag, but, because it wasn't zipped, a pile of books fell out. Melody scrambled to grab them, but Corona glanced down before she had time to shove them back into her book bag.

"My diaries." She reached down and grabbed one of the books. "You took my diaries?"

Tess sprang up from the edge of the bed. "Okay. And

this is when I exit stage left. C'mon, Mom. These two are going to need a moment alone."

Adele didn't know what was going on, but she allowed her youngest daughter to pull her from the bedroom.

Once they were gone, Corona glanced at her daughter. "Why do you have my diaries?"

"I was just… I sort of found them," she admitted.

"What makes you think that they were lost? Or that you had the right to take them?"

Melody lowered her head. "I shouldn't have taken them. I'm sorry."

Corona felt stripped. "You're sorry, or you're sorry that you got busted?"

"I'm… I guess that I got busted."

Corona shook her head as more tears spilled over her lashes. "These were personal…private." She reached over and took her daughter's book bag and saw four other books.

"You had so many of them, I didn't think that you'd notice they were gone," Melody said.

"So you read them?" It was sort of a foolish question at this point, but she asked it anyway.

Her daughter just bobbed her head. "I'm sorry."

"Please stop saying that." She tilted her head into the palm of her hand. Now where was she supposed to go with this conversation? And why did this hurt more than being dumped on national television and newspapers had?

"Momma?" Melody finally lifted her head. "Is Lyfe Alton my father?"

Chapter 24

Lyfe was amazed at the wall-to-wall coverage that the Rowan James and Danica Foxx reconciliation story was getting in just mere hours. Apparently not only had the two actors hooked up, but they'd hopped a plane to Monoco and had a quick wedding ceremony. Every station, from the entertainment networks to the news networks, was indulging in the scandal.

Lyfe was torn between two emotions. One on hand, this certainly cleared the field for him; and on the other hand, he was concerned about how Corona was taking the news. By noon, he couldn't stand it any longer and called her cell phone. The call went straight to her voicemail. He tried her office, but after charming Margo for about twenty minutes, he was told that her boss wouldn't be coming into the office today.

That only heightened his concern.

"I say go over there," Hennessey said. "If you're

trying to figure out where you fit in, then this is going to be your chance to step up and be the shoulder that she's going to need. Women love that stuff."

"I don't know," Royce countered. "Women also love their space. And after this scandal blowing up like this, she's probably looking for a big rock to hide under. You don't want to seem too eager, you know?"

Lyfe agreed with both brothers' points, so he was still torn as to what he should do. In the end, he took a poll among the Alton six-pack and found that they were split right down the middle. Three said go to her and three said to wait for her to come to him.

After another hour of coverage, he developed cabin fever and decided to take a long stroll. However, the minute he hit the streets, there were magazine and newspaper vendors with tabloids screaming the scandal on their front pages. The next thing he knew, he was hailing a cab.

The cab driver asked, "Where to?"

He drew a blank for a moment and then vaguely remembered Tess saying something about… "The Centurion?"

The cabbie nodded his head and took off. Within minutes, he was outside the luxury apartments and was stunned to see a number of photographers outside, smoking. Were they there hoping to get an exclusive shot of the recently dumped fiancée?

He shook that troubling thought from his head and raced inside the building, scooting behind another tenant who was entering the building. At the elevator, he helped an older lady enter with her wheelchair, and in her gratitude, she told him which apartment a Chloe Banks stayed in.

It wasn't until after he knocked on the door that he realized he didn't even know what to say if she answered. *Sorry about your breakup?* She would see straight through that lie. At the same time, he couldn't just stroll into her crib, grinning and ready to perform cartwheels.

At the sound of someone approaching the door, Lyfe decided to play it by ear. When the door opened, he pushed up a smile.

"Lyfe?" Tess's eyes bulged before she glanced out into the hallway as to see if he was alone. "What are you doing here?"

He grinned. "What do you think? I'm here to see your sister. I'm still pursuing her, remember?"

When his answer did nothing to erase the worry lines across her forehead, he grew a little more concerned. "Is Corona here?"

"Ohhh…uh…"

"Who's at the door, Tess?" Adele Banks's voice floated over.

Lyfe looked over Tess's head and smiled. "Good afternoon, Mrs. Banks."

The color drained from the older woman's face. "Lyfe? What are you doing here?" she asked him. She shot a sharp look at her youngest daughter.

"I'm here to see Corona Mae." Why did this exchange have him feeling like a teenager again? "Well, that's if Tess will let me in," he added.

"Uhhh…" Tess seemed to scramble for the right words. "Look, Lyfe. I know that I have been really pushing for you and my sister to get back together—"

"What? You've changed your mind?" he asked.

"No. No. I just think that *today* isn't a good day for—"

"Melody, please, wait!" Corona Mae called out, drawing everyone's attention.

"Mom, I have a right to know!" a young voice shouted out.

Mom? The wheels inside Lyfe's head screeched to a halt. "Corona has a daughter?" he asked. "How come you never told me?"

Tess glanced away.

"Just answer the question, Mom. Is this *Lyfe Alton* my father or isn't he?"

At those words, Lyfe felt the world tilt on its axis. He couldn't have heard that right. With hardly any effort, he shoved open the door and shoulder-bumped Tess out of the way.

Corona's head swiveled toward the door. Her eyes doubled in size. "Lyfe."

The teenage girl also jerked her head toward the door, and for the first time, father and daughter locked eyes.

"I know you," Melody said, her eyes narrowing. "I've seen you before."

In a flash, Lyfe remembered the cluster of teenagers that had bumped into him as he was coming out of the elevator about a week ago. He nodded. "I remember seeing you, too." His eyes shot over to Corona for some type of explanation.

But all he could see, besides the steady stream of tears flowing, was the face of deception. He shook his head as his heart shattered. Looking back over at the young girl, he recognized his eyes, his nose and even his jawline. "How old are you?"

"Thirteen."

The wind sailed out of Lyfe's chest as if he'd just been sucker punched. Once again his eyes zipped back to Corona Mae. "Is she…?"

"Lyfe…I, uh…I'm sorry." She came over to him, but he stepped back.

"You're sorry?" He looked back at the little girl…*his* little girl. She was still there. He wasn't imagining all of this. Still, he couldn't stop shaking his head. "You kept something like this from me?"

"I—I—"

"You had my *child* and you never said anything?" His accusatory glare swept around the room. "*None* of you said anything?"

Rufus Banks strolled out from another hallway. "What's going on out here?"

Lyfe was on a roll. "Now I expected something like this from *him!* But you, Corona?"

"It was like I told you the other night. We were young and—"

"It wasn't your decision to make," he roared. "I should've had a say in this!"

"I wanted to tell you but—"

"And in fourteen years, you couldn't find the time to pick up a phone—write a letter—send an email? Is that what I'm supposed to believe?"

"Adele and I didn't think it was our place," Rufus interjected.

"You once shot at me and then held a gun to me to marry your daughter, and then *suddenly* you had a revelation of what was and wasn't your place?"

"Lyfe, please." Corona raced over to him.

He started backpedaling toward the door. "You're unbelievable. How could you do something like this?"

"I thought it was the right thing to do."

"For who? You? Because you didn't want to be stuck in the same country town and marry a farmer? Your choice didn't have anything to do with me. It was all about you—and what *you* wanted. What did I ever do to deserve such disregard?"

Larger tears rolled down Corona's face as she trembled terribly.

"Did you know when you left that day? When you left me standing like an idiot at the altar in front of my family and friends?"

"No," she choked out. "I swear."

"And I should believe you because?"

Once again, Corona tried to erase the distance between them and reach out for him.

"Don't," he barked. "Don't touch me. I don't know you." He choked on those last words. "I thought I did, but…" Lyfe shook his head. "The woman I fell in love with would have never done something like this. Maybe…that was the problem all along. You were never the woman, or the girl, I thought you were." He turned. "I got to get out of here."

When he reached the door, Melody called out, "Wait!"

He froze.

Melody pushed past her mother to come up behind him. "I…I'd really like to get to know you."

Slowly, he pivoted around and exposed his own tears. "I'd like that very much." He reached into his jacket and pulled out a business card. "Call me. We'll talk and arrange something."

Melody smiled as she clutched the business card. "Thanks."

He nodded and, without sparing Corona another glance, he raced out of the door.

Chapter 25

"I believe that this belongs to you," Corona said, slipping off her ring and sliding it across her dining room table.

Rowan gave her an awkward smile. "Maybe you should keep it."

"What? So I can have something to remember you by?" she asked with her own smile. "That's all right. In the end, everything worked out for the best between us."

He nodded. "Are you going to call him?"

She'd confessed about her and Lyfe and what she'd been doing since he was off cavorting with Danica Foxx. She figured his interest in her and Lyfe was helping him with whatever guilt he still felt for his impromptu marriage.

"Call him and tell him what? That everything he said was right?"

"That's a start."

She shook her head. "I don't know. Right now I think I'm the last person he wants to see. But…I guess I should be grateful that whatever transpired between us isn't preventing him and Melody from developing a relationship. He wants her to go to Georgia for Christmas next week and meet her other family. She's practically bouncing off the walls with excitement."

Rowan reached a hand across the table. "I really do hope that everything works out for you."

Despite promising herself that she wasn't going to spend another day crying her eyes out, tears started to gather in rebellion.

"Well, I guess I better go," he said, standing up from the table.

She stood as well and then walked him to the door. "Good luck, Rowan." She leaned over and brushed a kiss against the side of his face. "I really do wish you and Danica the best."

"Thanks. I wish the best for you and your true love, as well."

Christmas was suddenly barreling toward Corona at warp speed. And before she knew it, it was time for her and Melody to pack for Georgia. She figured that, while Melody was getting acquainted with the Altons, she would spend Christmas at her parents'. A first in fourteen years.

They took an early morning flight then rented a car for the drive to Thomason.

Melody was over the moon. "Five uncles," she kept saying and shaking her head. "I hope that I'll be able to keep their names straight."

"If they're anything like I remember, you won't

have any problem distinguishing them for one another. Though they all are quite the pranksters."

"You mean like how they stole you and Dad's clothes when you went skinny dipping together?" Melody asked, chuckling.

Corona's ears burned with embarrassment. "I still can't believe you read my diaries."

"Aw. C'mon, Mom. I think it's kind of cool that you used to do stuff like that."

"Yeah. Well...don't let me hear about you doing that crazy stuff." She frowned.

Melody laughed. "You look like Grandpa Rufus when you make faces like that."

That was reassuring. She was turning into her parents. When she pulled their rental car into the Alton's driveway, she couldn't help but be transported back to the days when she spent as much time at this house as she had at her own.

"Okay, 'bye, Mom." Melody leaned over and pressed a kiss against her cheek and then hopped out of the car.

"You be good," she shouted, a second before the passenger door was slammed in her face. Nervously, she watched as her daughter raced up the wraparound porch to knock on the door.

A second later, it opened, and Lyfe stepped out in an over-the-top Christmas sweater with a yellow labrador barking at his heels. He quickly enveloped his daughter into his strong arms while a look of sheer delight covered his face. The sight of them together caused a new ocean of tears to gather at the back of Corona's eyes. She had been so wrong to keep the two of them apart. So very wrong.

Lyfe glanced over to the car and, for one brief second,

their eyes connected. The smile that he'd shared with his daughter faded at its edges, as hurt flickered in his eyes. Then just as quickly, he glanced away and escorted his daughter into the house, where she could meet her new family.

Dear Diary,
I know that it's been a while. But in my darkest hours you have always been a faithful and silent shoulder. I'm at a crossroads. I don't know how to correct a terrible wrong I've done to someone I love. Lyfe and Melody are trying to forge a new relationship together, and I'm left on the sidelines cheering them on. I know that this will be a good thing for my daughter. It's been a long time since I've seen her so happy. And her happiness is going to have to be enough for me.

Still, today when I saw Lyfe, he gave me a look that broke what was left of my heart. I won't ask for him to forgive me. That is asking for the impossible. But I have to say, that if I had it all to do over again, I would've married Lyfe fourteen years ago with my daddy's shotgun at his back. I would've had Melody and a dozen more babies with his eyes and his smile. And I would be proud today to say that I was the wife of a farmer, a gas station attendant or anything else he wanted to be. I have a feeling that I would be a hell of a lot happier than I am right now.

"Corona?" Tess inquired, dipping her head into her sister's old bedroom. "Are you all right?"

Corona glanced up and closed her diary. "Yeah. I'm fine."

Tess lingered at the door as if afraid to cross the threshold. "I'm so sorry," she said. "This is all my fault. I thought that if…I got you two together, that everything would work itself out. I figured that as crazy as Lyfe was about you that—"

"It wouldn't matter that I kept him from his daughter?"

Tess dropped her head. "Given how he's always felt about you…yeah, I really did. It just didn't go down like I planned."

"Things rarely do." Corona chugged in a deep breath. "But…if you hadn't put your nose where it didn't belong, I guess I would've put off telling Melody about her father until she was eighteen. That probably would've been an even bigger mistake."

"Soooo…does that mean that I'm forgiven?"

A small smile flickered at the corners of her lips. "Yeah. I guess so."

Tess bolted into the room and gave her sister a much needed big hug. But when she pulled away, she went right back to her old ways. "You know, there's still a chance that Lyfe may calm down and talk to you."

Corona Mae shook her head. "No. It's over," she said, remembering his face that afternoon. "He'll never forgive me for this one."

An hour later, Corona Mae sat swinging on her parent's porch swing, looking up at the blanket of stars while Christmas music still played inside. Every memory she'd ever shared with Lyfe in this small town scrolled through her head. It didn't seem so oppressive now that she'd lived in the big city. She sort of enjoyed how much slower and calmer life was out here.

Despite her being the talk of the town, everyone was still pleasant when they saw her—and most told her how beautiful her daughter was. She guessed that meant Lyfe was out showing her off like a proud father.

"Looks like you sprung a leak," her father said, stepping out onto the porch.

Corona Mae mopped at her eyes. "Hey, Daddy."

"Hey." He slid his hands into his pockets and then joined her on the swing. "I would ask how you're holding up, but after watching you trip over your bottom lip all day, I think I get the picture."

She smiled.

"You know, uh, I never got the chance to apologize for uhm…" He searched for the right words. "Well, I guess for ruining your life."

"What?" She twisted toward him.

He shrugged. "None of this would've happened if I hadn't overreacted when I saw you…in there…back then."

"Oh, Daddy. You didn't ruin my life."

"Didn't I? If it wasn't for me, then you would've never ran away from home, never had to try and raise that child on your own…who knows? In all likelihood, you and Lyfe would've gotten together in your own time." His eyes started glistening. "And if I wasn't so stubborn, I would've apologized long before now."

She reached over and took his hand. "It's all right, Daddy. Turns out that I overreacted too when I ran away."

"Does that mean that I'm forgiven?"

"Yes. Yes. A thousand times, yes. I love you, Daddy. I know that you only did what you thought was right."

"Thank you, baby. I really needed to hear that." He inched closer. "You have to forgive yourself as well."

Corona lowered her eyes. "I don't know if I deserve it."

"None of us deserves it, baby girl. But we all need it. I know it may surprise you to hear me say this, but Lyfe is a good man. And he would be so lucky to have you."

She shook her head. "He doesn't love me anymore."

"Nonsense. When a man loves a woman for as long as he has loved you, it will take a hell of a lot more than this to change it. He's just hurt right now. Go to him."

The tears started rolling faster again. "B-but he won't listen to me."

"Then we'll have to figure out a way to make him listen."

"I love you, Daddy."

"I love you too, baby girl."

She smiled and then launched herself into his arms. They held each other and cried.

Bright and early on Christmas morning, Corona Mae opened her eyes and immediately wondered how Melody was enjoying herself over at the Alton's house. No doubt that she would be smothered with Christmas gifts, which would probably take a week to pack and ship back to New York. For most of Christmas Eve, her daughter had texted photos of her and her new family. It looked as if half of Georgia had come down to see her.

"I'm happy for her," she whispered up to the ceiling.

"Rise and shine," Tess said, bursting into her room like she used to do when they were younger.

"Don't you know how to knock?" Corona groaned.

Tess turned back around and knocked on the open door. "Better?"

"Whatever." Corona rolled her eyes, picked up a pillow and then buried her head underneath it.

"Nah, huh. None of that. Time to get up. Time for presents."

Corona groaned.

Tess placed her hands on her waist. "How on earth do you run a big agency when I can't even get you out of bed?"

She lifted the pillow. "I'm on vacation!"

"No. You're working my nerves." She grabbed the pillow and tossed it across the room. "Now get up! Everybody is waiting."

"Not everybody. Melody isn't here."

"Melody is downstairs."

"What?" Corona finally jumped out of bed. "She's here? Is something wrong? What happened?" She didn't even wait for an answer before she shot out of her bedroom and raced downstairs. Sure enough, Melody was laughing in the kitchen with her grandma.

"Melody, baby. What are you doing here?" She grabbed her and wrenched her into a tight hug. "Oh, I've missed you so much."

"It's only been two days, Mom." She laughed.

"But why are you here?"

"We always spend Christmas together," Melody said. "I don't see why today has to be any different."

"Oh." Corona's squeezed her tighter, feeling her heart explode with love.

"Momma, I can't breathe."

"Ah, sorry." She released her but continued to give her a weepy puppy dog look.

"All right now. Y'all gonna have me crying in these pancakes. Go on now. Get out of my kitchen with all that carrying on."

"It's okay, Momma. We're going to stop crying now."

"Uh-huh," she said with a smile.

"So." Corona turned back to Melody. "How did you get over here?"

"Grandpa Rufus came and got me. Then he and my uncles helped load up your Christmas present in his truck."

"My Christmas present?"

"Yeah. It's downstairs in the basement."

"The basement?" She glanced over at her mother, who quickly returned her attention to her skillet. Corona turned toward Tess, but she was suddenly interested in the paint on the ceiling. "All right. I'll bite. I'll go look." She marched out of the kitchen with Melody following closely behind.

She slowly descended the staircase, bracing herself for the unexpected. However, nothing in the world could've prepared her for seeing Lyfe strapped down and tied to a chair.

"Oh, my God, what is going on?"

Royce, Hennessey, Dorian, Ace and Jacob all glanced up from their handiwork while her father lowered his shotgun.

"Morning, sweetheart," her father said. "You're up early."

"Hmmmp, hmmpft," Lyfe mumbled beneath his gag.

"You kidnapped him?" she asked, astonished.

"Well," her father said, adjusting the bill on his cap.

"The way we figured, you two were going to waste an awful lot of time being mad at each other. So me and the Alton boys here thought that we'd just speed up the process so you two can talk."

"Yeah," Hennessey said. "Lil man here was working our nerves with his bottom lip hanging out these past few days. We all know that you love each other, so y'all are going to stay down here until you work this thing out."

Corona shook her head while still trying to process it all. "Y'all can't do this."

They looked at each other. "Sure we can."

"And we got something for you, too." Ace held up some rope and then launched toward her.

Corona turned and attempted to take off up the stairs, but Ace and his brothers proved that they were still very athletic when they plucked her off the staircase as if she weighed nothing.

"Oh, no, sweetheart. We know that you're a runner. But this time, you're going to sit right over here next to your lover boy and work this out."

"Daddy! Do something!"

Rufus chuckled. "I am doing something, baby girl. Whose idea do you think this was?"

Another chair was produced and set next to Lyfe. Next thing she knew, she was being tied to the chair.

"Wait. Wait. You can't do this."

But apparently they could…and they did. When they were through, the five Alton brothers and her father smiled with great satisfaction.

"Now, you two talk," Rufus said. "We'll be back down here after we think you've worked this thing out."

"Daddy."

"I'm only doing what I think is best, baby girl." He winked and pressed a kiss against her forehead. He then walked over to Lyfe and removed his gag. "You two have fun." He turned and marched out of the basement with the Altons behind him in a single file.

At the staircase Melody gave her parents a sympathetic smile, but she was definitely in cahoots with her grandpa and uncles. A few seconds later, the door at the top of the stairs slammed shut, leaving Lyfe and Corona Mae all alone.

"It's official. Your father is positively insane!"

"And what about those five mountains you call brothers?" she charged back. "Clearly they've all taken a couple of trips over the cuckoo's nest too."

Lyfe shook his head. "I should've known that you would take their side."

"I'm not taking anyone's side. You might want to notice that I'm tied to a chair in the basement too. It's not exactly how I planned to spend my Christmas."

"Yeah. I believe that you were hoping to be on your honeymoon with Mr. Box-office by now."

She gasped at the low blow. "How dare you! Look, I get that you're mad. But that doesn't mean that I have to sit here while you hurl insults at me."

"Oh? Going somewhere, are you?"

"Look, I made a mistake! All I can do is apologize—but I honestly believe that I was doing the right thing at the time. I didn't set out to deliberately hurt you. Why would I do that?"

"I honestly don't know. Now I'm doubting everything that I *thought* I ever knew about you."

Even the second time around, the jab hurt. But this time Corona fought the tears that rushed her eyes. "I'm sorry you feel that way—because I still love everything about you."

Lyfe's jaw hardened as he twisted his head away.

"Look, I've made a lot of mistakes while trying to do the right thing. Do my intentions not count? How could I truly believe that you wanted to marry me when my father had a six-gauge pointed at your back?"

"Don't be ridiculous," he spat. "You knew how I felt about you. The whole town knew."

"Ridiculous?" she echoed. "I asked you that day, down here in this basement, if you really wanted to marry me."

"And I said yes!"

"No!" She shook her head, her eyes turning accusatory. "You never answered the question. You opened your mouth, but you couldn't give me an answer," she reminded him. "Then when I told you that we didn't have to go through with it, and that my father wouldn't really shoot you, you joked that since he'd already tried once, he wouldn't miss the second time. But you *never* answered the question."

Lyfe's face softened as he tried to review his own account of that conversation.

"I believe that you loved me like you said, but you weren't sure about marrying at that time either. We were young—too young. Don't you see? I loved you enough to set you free."

The room dripped with silence, but the tension was slowly ebbing away.

"When did you know?" he asked quietly. "About Melody? When did you know that you were pregnant?"

"Three months later. And I almost came back home. I honestly did. It was senior prom time here, and I heard that you were taking Leanne Henry. You were going on and enjoying your teenage life like I wanted—and, at the time, it seemed selfish and manipulative to just show up. We would've been right back where we started, but with more pressure to marry."

"So you chose to go it alone?" he asked dubiously.

"I was a teenager. What passed for logic then doesn't make sense now. But once I started down that path, I couldn't get myself to change course. If I couldn't come back when I was three months pregnant, I couldn't come with a newborn, or a one-year-old, or a ten-year-old, or a teenager." Corona Mae sniffed, but kept up the battle against her tears. "All I can do now is apologize. But I can tell you that there wasn't one day that I didn't think about you. There wasn't a single day that I didn't wonder where you were. Were you happy? Had I made the right decision? Just like there was hardly a night when I didn't think about that snowy night when we made love in front of the fireplace. It was one of the happiest moments of my life. My one joy was waking up every morning and staring into our daughter's eyes and seeing you."

Lyfe finally met her gaze and revealed his eyes glossed with tears. "I was scared that day," he admitted. "It was all going…so fast. But the one thing I knew when I showed up in that god-awful tuxedo was that I loved you. And at seventeen, I thought it was going to be enough. Maybe it was—maybe it wasn't. I guess we'll never know."

Corona Mae's bottom lip began to tremble. "What about now?" She sniffed as her tears started to gain ground. "Do you really hate me?"

"No," he said without hesitation. "Apparently that's impossible for me."

A bud of hope began to bloom. "Do you think that you can ever forgive me?"

"I already have. I think that's why I'm mad at myself." He chuckled.

It wasn't enough. She pushed on. "Do you think you can ever love me again?"

"I've never stopped. I think that's another reason why I was mad at myself." To her surprise, the rope fell from his wrists, and he quickly unbound his legs.

"How?"

"Royce never could tie a good sailor's knot." He got up, untied her, and then kneeled by her chair. "I've wanted to do this for fourteen years."

He reached into his pocket and withdrew a beautiful two-carat ring. "Corona Mae Banks, will you marry me?"

Tears poured down her face and she shouted, "Yes. A million times, yes!"

Their arms flew around each other and their lips melded together.

The basement door burst open with celebratory whoops as the Alton men raced down the stairs in black tuxedos.

"Looks like today is a good day for a wedding," Royce shouted.

"What?" Corona Mae jerked her head back toward Lyfe.

He smiled mischievously. "All right. So maybe...I wasn't *exactly* kidnapped."

"Oh, you!" She smacked him on the chest.

Bringing up the rear was their daughter in an elegant

pink-lace dress. "Momma, we got to get you up to your room so you can get dressed. You don't want to be late for your own wedding."

Corona Mae's smile continued to stretch. "I wouldn't miss this one for the world."

Epilogue

December 25, 2014
Dear Diary,
It's hard to believe that today Lyfe and I celebrated our second wedding anniversary. Where has the time gone? Maybe this is just how it is when one is truly happy. I don't even miss my former life in New York. How could I when every morning I wake up surrounded by love? But today was extra special. After we made love by the fireplace, I told Lyfe that he was going to be a father again.

I had a chance to tell Melody about the baby yesterday, and she's as ecstatic as her father. It's amazing how much of a daddy's girl she is now. My move back to Thomason has also allowed me and my father to heal, and I'm now as much a daddy's girl as my daughter.

Melody loves spending her Saturdays hunting and fishing and playing pool. She's also the pride and joy of her five uncles, and all of them have been threatening every boy that comes within a mile of her. I think having a girl in their tight clan has changed those Alton boys' attitudes toward women as well. One can only hope.

After Lyfe quit his architecture firm, he started a consultant business that he runs from home, and we also started our own grass-fed farm with free-range chickens. Turns out, it's a booming business now that there's such a local farm movement.

As for Tess, I think there's something going on between her Hennessey. Those pranksters are like two peas in a pod—only they're the only ones who don't notice how alike they are.

We'll see.

* * * * *

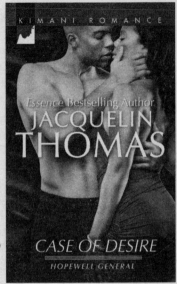

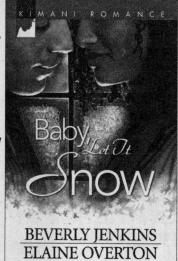

REQUEST YOUR FREE BOOKS!

2 FREE NOVELS
PLUS 2 FREE GIFTS!

KIMANI™
ROMANCE

Love's ultimate destination!

KROM11B

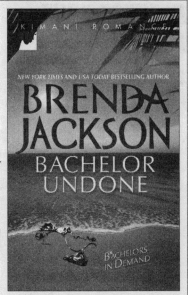